An Heir for the Millionaire
He will claim what is rightfully his!

With a wolfish smile and a sexy glint in his eye,
he never fails to achieve the impossible.

When he discovers he is about to become a
father, this proud, determined millionaire will
stop at nothing to claim his heir...and his woman!

Two gorgeous men called Xander,
two explosive stories!

Treat yourself to a dose of pure passion,
drama and excitement, brought to you by two of
your favorite Presents® authors, Julia James and
Carole Mortimer.

2 Stories in 1

Julia James
Carole Mortimer
AN HEIR FOR THE MILLIONAIRE

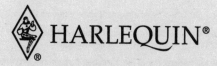

HARLEQUIN®

TORONTO • NEW YORK • LONDON
AMSTERDAM • PARIS • SYDNEY • HAMBURG
STOCKHOLM • ATHENS • TOKYO • MILAN • MADRID
PRAGUE • WARSAW • BUDAPEST • AUCKLAND

ISBN-13: 978-0-373-12936-2

AN HEIR FOR THE MILLIONAIRE
Copyright © 2010 by Harlequin Books S.A.

First North American Publication 2010.

The publisher acknowledges the copyright holders
of the individual works as follows:

THE GREEK AND THE SINGLE MOM
Copyright © 2007 by Julia James.
Previously published in the U.K. as *The Greek and the Single Mum*

THE MILLIONAIRE'S CONTRACT BRIDE
Copyright © 2008 by Carole Mortimer.

Recycling programs
for this product may
not exist in your area.

This edition published by arrangement with Harlequin Books S.A.

For questions and comments about the quality of this book
please contact us at Customer_eCare@Harlequin.ca.

® and ™ are trademarks of the publisher. Trademarks indicated with
® are registered in the United States Patent and Trademark Office, the
Canadian Trade Marks Office and in other countries.

www.eHarlequin.com

Printed in U.S.A.

CONTENTS

THE GREEK AND THE SINGLE MOM

Julia James

PROLOGUE

CLARE took a deep breath and walked forward into the dimly lit cocktail bar. Soft music issued from the white piano in the corner, and she vaguely recognised an old number from the fifties. But she paid it no attention, heading instead for the nearest table, set low and surrounded by deep leather easy chairs designed to soothe the bodies of besuited businessmen, weary from a hard day's work in the corridors of power.

Her mouth twisted slightly. Those corridors—and the board-rooms and suites that opened off them—might demand long hours, but they also awarded a de luxe lifestyle to those who stalked them. Bespoke suits, handmade shoes, perfect grooming, and the ability to pay exorbitant prices with a flick of a platinum credit card.

As Clare approached the table, around which a cluster of suits eased back in the armchairs, a soft, throaty laugh made her turn her head slightly. A little way away, at another table, a couple sat on a sofa, drinks in hand. It was not the man who had laughed so seductively, but his female companion. For a brief moment Clare allowed herself to look. Even in the soft lighting she could see that the woman was very beautiful, with chic hair, expertly styled, and immaculate make-up. Her dress was a designer number, and clung to her lissom form. As she gave her soft laugh, she crossed her long, sheer-stockinged legs, and one elegantly manicured hand hovered over her companion's thigh.

A little stab went through Clare. She looked away.

I shouldn't have taken this job. I knew it was a mistake!

For four long years she had kept away from places like this. The world she lived in now was in a different universe. Stepping back into this lush, expensive environment was not something she had wanted to do.

It brought back too many memories.

And the brief glimpse of that designer-clothed female had intensified them.

Was I ever really like that?

It seemed impossible—and yet with her brain she knew it was true. She too, once, a lifetime ago, had been like that woman. Beautifully clothed, immaculately made up, elegant and chic.

She inhaled sharply. What did it matter that this place brought back the past? Memories she didn't want and didn't welcome. She was here simply because it was the best way she had of making the extra money she needed if her determination to take Joey and her friend Vi on holiday that summer was to succeed. Evening work was the only kind that was possible, and waiting cocktail tables in this swish new hotel, recently opened on an arterial road *en route* to Heathrow in West London, a bus ride away from where she lived with Vi, had to be a lot better than working in a pub, or in her local pizza parlour.

As for the memories its luxury triggered—well, tough. Her chin lifted. She'd have to get over it.

The uncompromising injunction resonated in her head. *Get over it.* One of the toughest self-help commandments around— and yet it had helped her, she knew, during those four long years. Years when she'd had to completely change her life—not just her lifestyle, but something far more profound. Far more difficult.

No. *Don't go there!*

That was another maxim she'd had to rigidly cling to. Don't go there—where in her dreams, her yearnings, she longed to go. Back into the past. A past that ached like an old, deep, unhealable wound.

Or, worse, don't go into a present that did not exist—a parallel universe of longing and desire that was conjured up out of her deepest places, where the choice she had made had been quite, quite different.

Well, I didn't make that choice! I chose a different way. And it was the right way to choose—the only way.

However hard the choice had been, it would have been far worse if she hadn't made it. She'd paid the price for her decision, and even to think of it was agonising…just agonising.

Her own voice interrupted her painful thoughts.

'Good evening, gentlemen—what may I get you to drink?'

Painting a bright, attentive smile on her face, she listened and nodded and scribbled as fast as she could, hoping she was getting it down right. She headed back to the bar to relay the order.

'Doing OK?' asked Tony, one of the barmen, congenially.

'I hope so,' Clare replied cautiously.

He wasn't to know that it was not just her being new to the job that was making her cautious. That the whole expensive ambience of the place was disturbing her. Threatening her with memories of a life she had once led, and which was gone for ever. At least she'd never been at this place before; she was more familiar with the classic de luxe hotels, like the Savoy in London and the Plaza in New York. This hotel was too new, too impersonal, not at all the kind that—

She spotted a customer beckoning her and hurried across, glad of the distraction. Glad, too, that she was kept on her feet without respite as the evening wore on. Her feet in the unaccustomed high heels were starting to ache, but apart from a couple of confusing moments regarding complicated cocktails she was basically coping, she thought. She was careful always to keep her physical distance from the guests, but by and large she wasn't getting any hassle.

But then, of course, she acknowledged, with part relief and partly a little pang, the closest she got to a beauty treatment these days was filing a hang nail…

But what did she care? she thought fiercely. Joey didn't give a hoot if her hair was just tied back in a utilitarian plait, or if her face was bare of make-up. All he wanted was her attention—and her love.

And he got both in infinite amounts.

Even as she thought of Joey her hand automatically went to

her apron pocket. Her mobile was on, but there had been no peep from it. Vi still found it tricky to use a mobile, but she'd made a gallant effort to learn, and had faithfully promised to call Clare if Joey surfaced and was distressed at her absence in any way. But, with luck, Joey was a good sleeper now, and once he went off he was usually fine until morning.

She handed round the drinks she'd just collected from the bar, spotted another of her tables starting to disperse, and kept an eye on them to see if she was going to get a tip. The wages, like all in this line of work, were hardly brilliant, and tips were important, like it or not. Every penny counted, and every penny was going into the Holiday Jar that would, she fervently hoped, take her and Joey and Vi to the seaside in the summer.

A shadow formed in her eyes.

If fate had dealt her a different card there'd be no such thing as the Holiday Jar...

But it was no use thinking that way. She had made the right choice, the only choice.

This way, though Joey might only be the fatherless child of yet another impoverished single mother, wearing clothes out of charity shops and eking a living, that was still infinitely better than being the alternative—the unwanted bastard of a Greek tycoon and his discarded, despairing mistress...

CHAPTER ONE

XANDER ANAKETOS stifled his impatience with a civil, if brief smile at the man beside him. Richard Gardner was of the school of businessmen who considered that every deal should be sealed with a drink and an expensive meal. Xander had no time for such niceties. The investment he'd just agreed in principle to make in Gardner's company would be mutually profitable, and the details would be hammered out by their respective subordinates. Now Xander was eager to be gone. He had plans for the evening which did not include making small talk with Richard Gardner. However, he had no wish to snub the older man, and besides, his 'other business' would wait for him.

They always waited for him.

Sonja de Lisle was no exception.

Oh, she might pout for a few minutes, but it wouldn't last. Soon she would be purring all over him. He pulled his mind away. Best not to let his thoughts go to Sonja when he had dinner to get through first.

And before that a drink in the cocktail lounge while they perused the menu.

As the guest, Xander let Gardner choose where to sit, and took his place accordingly. He glanced round, concealing the disparagement in his eyes. This was not a hotel he would have chosen to patronise, but he could appreciate that it was convenient for the business park where Gardner's company was sited near Heathrow. But, for himself, he preferred hotels to have more class, more prestige—usually more antiquity. He liked classic, world-famous hotels, like the Ritz, Claridges, the St John.

Memory flickered. He rarely went to the St John now.

Like a stiletto sliding in between his synapses, an image came into his mind. Blonde hair, curving in a smooth swathe over one shoulder, diamond studs set into tender lobes, long dark lashes and cool grey-green eyes.

Eyes that were looking at him without emotion. A face held very still.

A face he had not seen again.

He thrust the image aside. There was no point remembering it.

Abruptly he reached for the menu that had been placed on the low table in front of them and flicked it open, making his selection without great enthusiasm. Snapping it shut, he tossed it down on the table again and looked around impatiently. He could do with a drink. Did this place not run to waitresses?

There was one a table or so away from them with her back to him. He kept his eye on her, ready to beckon. He could see her nodding, sliding her notepad into her pocket.

She turned towards the bar. Xander held up an imperious hand. She caught the gesture and altered direction.

Then she stopped dead.

Clare could feel the blood and all sensation slowly draining out of her body. It emptied from her brain, her limbs, every part of her, draining down through every vein, every nerve.

And in its place only two things.

Disbelief.

And memory.

Memory…

Poisonous. Toxic. Deadly.

And completely overwhelming.

She was dragged in its wake, down, down, down through the sucking vortex of time.

Down into the past…

Xander was late.

Restlessly, Clare paced up and down. She should by now be

used to him arriving when he wanted to, but this time it was harder to bear. A lot harder. She could feel nerves pinching in her stomach. Every muscle was tightly clenched.

Am I really going to tell him?

The question stung in her mind for the thousandth time. For two weeks it had been going round and round in her head. And with every circulation she knew that there was only one answer—could only be one answer.

I've got to tell him. I can't not.

And every time she told herself that she would feel the familiar flood of anxiety pooling in her insides—the familiar dread.

If—she corrected herself—*when* she told him, how would he take it? Automatically, in her head, she felt herself start to pray again. *Please, please let him take it the way I so desperately want him to! Please!*

But would he? Like a lawyer, she tried to shore up her position as best she could, mentally arranging all her arguments like ducks in a row.

I've lasted longer than the others. That has to be a good sign, doesn't it?

Xander Anaketos never kept his mistresses long. She knew that. Had known it since before that fateful night when she had joined their long, long list. But she hadn't cared. Hadn't cared that her shelf-life in his bed was likely to be in the order of six months, if that. Hadn't cared even that she'd got that fact from one of the most reliable sources for such information—her predecessor. Aimee Decord had warned her straight. The woman had been drunk, Clare knew, though it had hardly showed except for the slightest swaying in her elegant walk, the slightest lack of focus in her dark, beautiful eyes.

'Enjoy him, *cherie*,' she'd said to Clare, taking yet another sip of her always full champagne flute. 'You'll be gone by Christmas.' Her smile had almost had a touch of pity in it, as well as malice. And something more—something that had not been jealousy, but something that had chilled Clare even more than jealousy would have. A despairing hunger…

But Aimee Decord had been wrong. Clare had not been gone

by Christmas. Indeed, she'd spent the holiday with Xander in Davos, skiing. Just as she'd spent the last two weeks of January in the Caribbean, and Easter in Paris. Followed by a tour of North America, taking in New York, Chicago, San Francisco, Vancouver and Toronto—a hectic schedule which had whirled her along in the wake of one business meeting after another. Then it had been back to Europe, a sojourn in Paris again, then Geneva, Milan, another brief, but so very precious holiday in the Caribbean, and back to London.

Six months—nine months. Nearly a year. Very nearly a year.

In fact, Clare knew to the day—the night!—that in three weeks it would be their anniversary. And by then—oh, please, sweet God—by then she would have more to celebrate than that.

She went on pacing restlessly. Nerves still pinching. Still running through the tangled, shadowy fantasies that might or might not prove true.

It wasn't just that she'd lasted nearly twice as long as other mistresses of Xander Anaketos. Or that he had never installed her in an apartment, as he had the others, preferring that she should accompany him on his constant travels to the continents on which he conducted his complex and never-ending business affairs in the mysterious and arcane realm of international finance. Clare knew nothing about it, and did not enquire, having realised very early on that when Xander did finally clock off from business he wanted no more discussion of it until he was recalled to its demands.

There was another fantasy, most precious of all, that had came true recently, and which she now hugged to herself with a desperate hope.

Their last time together, nearly a fortnight ago, had been different. She'd known it—felt it. At first she'd thought it was only herself, suffused, as she had been, body and heart, with the knowledge that she possessed about what had happened to her so completely and absolutely unexpectedly, and yet so thrillingly.

But the change had not just been in her, she knew—*knew*. Xander had been different too. Oh, he'd been as passionate as ever, as voracious in his desires and needs, and as dedicated to fulfilling her own physical needs, desires. But there had been something more—more than could be accounted for merely because he had not seen her for ten days and had, the moment he'd stepped through the door, tossed aside his briefcase and swept her into his arms, carrying her off to his bed even while he was removing her clothes and devastating her with his kisses, the kisses of a man deprived for too long of what he most wanted.

The flames had consumed them, as they always did, bathing them like writhing salamanders in the fire of passion. But afterwards…ah, afterwards…Clare shut her eyes, shivering with remembered emotion. He had gone on holding her, tightly, closely, fervently. His hand had slid around her head, spearing through her hair, pressing her into his shoulder, while his other arm had wrapped around her like a clamp. She had heard, against her breast, the tumultuous pounding of his heart, felt her own beating against his.

He had said words to her in Greek and then fallen silent. She'd gone on lying crushed against him, her heart so full, *so full*. Then his hand had left her waist, and his other hand the back of her head, and he had shifted to cup her head with both his hands, one either side, and she'd half lifted herself from him.

She'd gazed down into his face. The face she knew so intimately, so absolutely. Every line, every plane, every lean contour, every sooty lash, every indentation around his sculpted, mobile mouth. He'd stared into her eyes from the depths of his own dark, midnight eyes, and there had been something in the way he'd looked at her that had made her heart turn slowly over.

He'd said another word in Greek. She hadn't known what it meant, hadn't cared, had only gazed down into his eyes, her heart slowly turning over, like a satellite in space, dissociated from the common earth.

It was that look, that long, endless exchange, that she clung to now. It had become a symbol, a beacon that she was now about to test her fate upon.

He cares for me. I know he does. It's not just the consideration of a lover, the conventional courtesy of a man towards his mistress. It's more than that.

How much more she did not know, dared not hope. But there

was something there—a seed, nothing more as yet, but enough, oh, enough for her to feast on!

But she must not feast—she must be frugal in her hope. And she must not, *must not*, seek to harvest it before it had time to grow, blossom to fruition.

Automatically she paused in her pacing, lifting her hand to her abdomen, and placing it there. She felt, as always, emotion welling up in her. So much depended on that harvest.

If he cares for me then it will be all right. It will all be all right.

But what if she were wrong? Chill shuddered through her.

Too much depended on his reaction. Her whole life. Her whole future.

And not just hers.

Again, in an instinctive gesture as old as time, she cupped her abdomen.

'It will be all right,' she whispered to herself.

Clare went off to the kitchen to make herself a cup of calming herb tea. The kitchen—fearsomely modern—still made her breath catch whenever she went in. So did the whole apartment— but then so did Xander's apartment in Paris, not just the one here in London, and the one in Manhattan.

She still found it strange that he seemed to have no fixed abode anywhere. Nowhere he called home.

But then, neither did she. Since her father's death two years ago she had had no home. Both her parents had been only children, and her mother had died when she was thirteen. The tragedy had thrown her and her schoolteacher father very close together, and his death from a long drawn-out cancer, when she was twenty, had been devastating.

And it had made her vulnerable. Susceptible. With the death of her father she had been entirely on her own. She had gone back to college, her studies having been interrupted when her father's illness had demanded full-time care, but her heart had not been in them. She had gone to London, preferring the anonymity of a huge city, far away from everything familiar and painful. The casual come-and-go of city life had suited her, teeming with people, none of them important to her, or her to them. She had taken temporary jobs, undemanding and unimportant, her emotions completely on hold after all the trauma of her father's death.

And then, without the slightest expectation, her emotions had sprung to life again. Vividly, terrifyingly alive. Alive in every nerve, every sense, every shimmering awareness.

Because of one man. She could remember in absolute detail the moment she had first seen him.

Clare had been sent by her temping agency to cover for a sick receptionist, and on her very first day, as she was sitting behind a plush, modernist-style desk, a covey of suited men had swung in through the doors. Her eyes had gone to them automatically— and stalled.

The man at the centre of the group had been the most arresting male she had ever seen—she hadn't been able to take her eyes from him.

He'd been tall, easily six foot, and lithe, and lean. His suit had been fantastically cut, making him look smooth and svelte and…devastating. And that was even before she'd registered the rest of him.

The sable hair, the tanned Mediterranean skin, the jaw-droppingly good-looking features.

And the eyes.

Eyes to drown in.

He had walked right past her with his entourage, unchallenged by the security guard, who had merely said in a respectful tone, 'Good afternoon, Mr Anaketos.' But just as he'd swung past her, sitting there staring at him, his head had suddenly moved minutely and brought his gaze to her. Abruptly, instinctively, she had twisted her head away…

They had gone past, and she had breathed out again, not even aware till then that she'd been holding her breath.

She had felt alive for the first time in a long, long time. As if she had woken from a long sleep…

It had been stupid, she knew, to have done thereafter what she had done. She'd been a woman rendered incapable of behaving rationally, but she had done it all the same. She had let Xander Anaketos seduce her.

And he had done it with a swiftness that had cut the ground out from under her feet. Before the week was out she had been flying to Geneva with him. How had he done it? She still did not know. She had done her best not to react to him whenever she had seen him, and even when he had paused by the reception desk to have a word with the security guard she had assiduously paid attention only to her computer screen. Yet on the day she'd been due to finish the posting, she had been summoned by phone to Xander's executive office on the top floor, where he had coolly invited her to dinner that night.

She had stared blankly.

'I'm afraid I don't think—' she had begun. Then stopped. Her chest had seemed tight. Xander Anaketos had been looking at her. She'd felt her toes start to melt into her shoes.

So she had gone.

And from dinner she had gone to his bed.

Should she have done it? Done something she had never done before—slept with a man on her very first date with him? She had. She had gone to his apartment, his bed, as unhesitatingly as if she'd had no conscious thought. But then she *hadn't* had any conscious thought about it. It had been instinct, an urge, an over-whelming, irresistible desire, that had made it impossible, utterly impossible, to say no, to stop the evening, to back away from him.

So she hadn't. She'd been able to do nothing but stand there, her whole body trembling with an intensity that she had never, ever experienced before, while Xander Anaketos walked across his vast apartment lounge towards her and slid one hand around the nape of her neck, caressing it lightly, oh so lightly, so sensu-ously, while his other hand slid long, skilled fingers into her hair and drew her mouth to his.

She had drowned. Fathoms deep.

Falling deep, deep into that wondrous, blissful world she still dwelt in now.

Or did she? Again, the strained look haunted her eyes again. Living with Xander was bliss—but it came with a price. She had learnt swiftly to start paying that price. Learnt it the first time she had taken Xander's hand in a spontaneous gesture of affection in public. He had disengaged and gone on talking to the person he'd been speaking to. She hadn't done it again. Nor did she ever put her hand on his sleeve, or lean against him, or show any other similar demonstration of affection. She had learnt not to do so, adopting instead the cool composure that he evidently preferred. In private he was passionate—thrillingly so!—taking her in a sensual storm, time after time, leaving her overwhelmed with emotion. Yet even in that white-out of exquisite sensation, and in the exhausted, replete aftermath as she lay limp in his arms, she knew better than to say to him what her heart urged her to say.

That she was, and had been even from their very first time together, hopelessly in love with him.

But she could never tell him. She knew that—and accepted it. He was a man who was essentially a loner, she recognised. He had made his own way in life, she knew, amassing his fortune through skill, daring and formidable financial acumen. Brought up by an elderly uncle, a professor of maths at a provincial Greek university, who had died some years ago, Xander had put his energies into his work. Clare knew that for Xander women were only for recreation and sexual pleasure, fleeting companionship, nothing more. He did not want emotional attachment. Let alone love.

But in the year they had been together he had shown no sign of restlessness with her, no sign of growing bored and weary of her. It was the reverse, if anything—especially that last, most precious time when they'd made love. She had sensed in the depths of her being that something was different between them.

She felt her heart catch again. Fill with hope again. Surely she was more than just the latest in his endless parade of mistresses who, as she had so swiftly learned, never engaged him for more than a handful of months at a time? He found it hard to express his emotions, she knew, preferring passion and sensuality—but that did not mean he did not feel them! Did not mean he felt nothing for her beyond physical attraction!

Again she replayed in her mind the memory of how he had

been different last time, how he had held her, gazed into her eyes, spoken those words to her in Greek that he had never said before… And yet again came hope, searing and urgent.

There was the sound of the apartment door opening. She felt her heart leap, then quiver, her eyes going immediately to where he would walk into the reception room.

And then he was there, paused in the entrance, his figure tall and familiar, making her breath catch in her lungs as it always did, every time she saw him again after an absence.

For a second her eyes lit, and for the briefest moment she was sure she saw an answering expression in his eyes.

Then it was gone.

'Delays at JFK,' he said. 'Then the motorway was jammed.' Xander gave an irritated shake of his head and set his briefcase down on the sideboard.

Clare stood, poised in the centre of the room. He turned to look at her. For a second there was that look in his eyes again, and then it was gone once more.

'I'll take a shower, then we can go out and eat,' he said.

Her eyes flickered. 'You don't want to eat here?'

He gave another cursory shake of his head. 'I've reserved the St John.'

'Oh. That's lovely,' Clare answered.

It might be lovely—the restaurant at the St John had become one of her favourites—but it was also unusual. Usually when Xander got back from abroad he preferred to eat in.

After sweeping her off to bed…

She looked at him uncertainly. He was loosening the knot of his tie, but he made no move towards her. Instead, he headed to the bedroom.

'Fix me a drink, will you, Clare?' he called.

She headed back to the kitchen and extracted a chilled bottle of beer from the fridge, opening it carefully and filling a glass. She made her way down to the en suite bathroom. He was already in the shower cubicle, and she could see his tall, naked body dimly behind the screen through the steam. He was washing his hair and had his back to her.

She left his drink on the vanity, and went into the bedroom. If they were going to the St John she'd better dress accordingly.

She had learnt very early on that Xander did not care to be kept waiting. He was never uncivil, but she could sense his irritation. The irritation of a rich man who didn't have to wait for things, or people. Including herself. So now she simply slipped on a dark green sheath, one of her favourites, brushed out her hair and retouched her make-up. Then she stepped back to check her appearance.

The familiar svelte, classically beautiful image looked back at her—hair smooth, make-up restrained, cool and composed.

She was still extremely slim. Nothing showed at all. Yet she could feel a distinct tightness in the dress fabric that was noticeable only by touch, not sight. Instinctively, yet again, she slipped her hand across her abdomen. Protectively. Cherishingly. A soft look came into her eyes.

Oh, let it be all right—please, please let it be all right!

The St John's three-Michelin-starred restaurant was as busy as ever, but for Xander Anaketos one of the best-positioned tables was always available. It was set back, in a quieter spot, although the hushed tones of the other diners made anyone else's conversation quite inaudible.

They took their places, and Clare knew that the eyes of the women there had gone to Xander—because women's eyes always did. And so did hers. After ten days of his absence, just drinking in his face, his features, running her eyes over the high slice of his cheekbones, lingering on the way his sable hair feathered, the way the lines around his mouth indented, was bliss.

She was glad now he had not swept her off to bed. In that sensual ecstasy she might not have been able to control her feelings for him, and in the aftermath she might have been tempted, oh, so tempted, to tell him what had happened. But it would not have been the right time, she knew. His mind, when he was in bed with her, was on sex—it was natural for a man, after all—and afterwards another hunger would take precedence, and he would suddenly want dinner. No. Better, she knew, to let him eat now, relax, chill from the irritations of the flight and let his mood mellow. And then, over brandy, she would tell him. It would be perfect.

The familiar stab of anxiety came again, but she dispelled it. There was no point in doing otherwise. She must think the best, hope the best. And in the meantime she must make it easy for him to relax. So she did what she always did—was poised and composed, chatting lightly, only in answer to him, not plaguing him, giving him time to eat, to let the fine wines slip down his throat, making no demands on him.

He was preoccupied, she could see. That was not unusual in itself. The demands of his work were immense, the convolutions of his myriad deals and negotiations, investments and financial manoeuvrings intricate and labyrinthine. In the early days she had asked him about his work, for the world of international finance was completely strange to her. She'd looked a bit up on the Internet and in newspapers, to try and be less of an ignoramus, but when she'd asked him about things he'd either looked wryly at her or told her that he had enough of it all day and wanted to relax now. So she'd accepted that and changed the subject.

Her eyes flickered to him again, as he focussed on his entrée. Yes, he was definitely preoccupied, his mind somewhere else. Quietly, she got on with her meal. She was hungry. Eating in the mornings now had little appeal, but by the evening she had worked up an appetite. However, she was very cautious about what she drank—her single glass of wine was still half full, and she was only taking tiny sips from it. She hadn't made a big deal out of it, and Xander hadn't remarked on it. Usually she drank a glass of white, and then red, and sometimes had a small liqueur afterwards, while he nursed a brandy. Tonight she would make do with coffee only.

Her mind, she found, was running on. She would need to buy a good comprehensive manual, she knew, and start finding out everything that was going to be in store for her now. It was such a complicated, overwhelming process, with her body and her psyche going through such profound changes. Physically, she felt wonderful—except for that distinct reluctance to eat first thing— but that might well change, she knew, over the coming months.

Another wave of unease went through her. Her figure would change totally, obviously, and what would Xander think? She'd always been so slim, so slender. How would he take the swelling of her body? Well, she would cope with it when the time came. It was only in the last trimester that the weight really piled on, and until then, if she kept fit, as she obviously must now, she should not look too bad. Her eyes softened. Xander might actually find her roundedness appealing…

Again, hope pierced her.

The meal continued, with both of them refusing dessert, and Xander ordering coffee and liqueurs.

'Just coffee for me, please.' Clare smiled at the waiter.

She felt Xander's eyes flicker over her a moment. Then it was gone again.

The coffee arrived, with his customary cognac, and the waiter departed again. The restaurant was thinning out now, the hushed voices more subdued. She watched as Xander cradled his glass in his long fingers and swirled it absently, his eyes going to the slow coil of topaz liquid within.

She felt her pulse quicken and took a breath. Now she must tell him. It was the right moment. She must not put it off. Nothing would be gained by doing so. Yet for an instant she desperately did not want to say anything! Wanted to put it off, procrastinate, delay what she must tell him.

She opened her mouth, his name forming on her lips.

'Clare.'

His voice came before hers. Her name. Clipped, pronounced.

Slowly her mouth closed, and she looked at him. Inside, emotions warred. One was dismay that he had spoken just as she was going to—but the other was sneaking and sly. She didn't have to tell him just yet…

Her eyes rested on him expectantly, waiting for him to continue. But there was a hesitation about him—something she was not used to seeing.

'Yes?' she prompted. Her voice was cool, composed, the way it always was—except in the throes of passion, when she cried out his name in ecstasy. 'What is it?'

Something shadowed in his eyes, and was gone. He swirled the brandy once more, then lifted it to his mouth and took a slow mouthful, lowering the glass. The air of preoccupation had vanished. There was a set in his shoulders, a tightening in his jaw. She looked at him, wondering what he was going to say to her. Wondering, far more anxiously, whether it would mean that telling him her news now would be delayed beyond this evening.

For a second longer he was silent. Then his eyes went to hers. There was no expression in them.

'I've met someone else. In New York.'

She heard the words. They were flatly spoken, his accent hardly showing. For a strange, dissociated moment she did not understand them.

Then he was talking again.

'There's never a pleasant way of doing this, but I wanted you to know how very much I've appreciated you over these last months. But it is now…' Did he hesitate again, just for a fraction of a fraction of a second? She could not tell, was blind and deaf to everything. 'Over,' he said, breathing out with a short, decisive breath.

She was sitting there. Just sitting there. Everything around her seemed to have gone into immense slow motion. As if it was not there. Was not there at all.

Her heart rate had slowed. She could feel it, slowing down like a motor running out of motion. Everything stilled inside her, around her, in the whole universe.

Her face did not move. That had stopped as well. Nor did her eyes. They were still looking at him. Just looking at him.

His eyes had a veiled look to them, and she could see his lips press together, as if in irritation. And as she went on just looking at him, because everything in the entire universe had just stopped, the line of irritation strengthened.

Then, abruptly, it was gone. He was moving, sliding his hand into his jacket pocket and gliding out a long, slim case. He placed it in front of her with a precise movement.

'As I said—' his voice still had that strange clipped quality to it '—I've appreciated you very much, and this is a token of that appreciation.'

Slowly, very slowly, as if there were lead weights on them, she pulled her eyes down to the slim jeweller's case in front of her, beside her coffee cup. Slowly she lifted her hands and opened the case. A long line of white fire glinted at her.

Diamonds, she thought. These are diamonds. A diamond necklace. For me.

He was talking again. His words came and went. She could hear snatches, as if through a thick, impenetrable fog.

'Naturally I don't want you to have any immediate concerns about accommodation. So I've taken an apartment for you, which is yours for the next month. That should give you ample time to make alternative arrangements—'

The words were coming and going, coming and going...

In strange, dissociated slow motion, she felt herself stand up.

'Clare?' His words had broken off. Her name came sharply.

'Will you excuse me a moment?' she said. Her eyes drifted to his. He seemed very far away. As far away as a distant star.

She felt for her handbag and walked away from the table. It was the strangest feeling—feeling nothing. That was what was so strange about it. Walking through a fog of nothingness.

She found the Ladies' and went inside. There was no one else there. For a moment she just looked at herself in the mirror above the row of gleaming basins.

She was still there. That was odd. She'd thought she had gone. That everything had gone.

But she was still there.

She blinked a moment. Her fingers closed around her clutch bag. For one moment longer she just looked at herself in the mirror. There was the faintest scent of lilies in the air, from the massive bouquet that adorned one of the vanity units to the side.

A sudden, hideous spurt of nausea leapt in her throat.

She turned on her heel.

The door swung open in her hand, and she was in the carpeted corridor outside. To her left was the way back to the restaurant. To her right the corridor led to a side entrance to the hotel that opened into a quiet street off the main West End thoroughfare the St John was situated on.

Her feet walked to the street door. It swung open at her touch.

Outside, on the pavement, the night air should have felt chill. But she did not feel it. She did not feel anything.

She started to walk.

CHAPTER TWO

CLARE had not seen him again from that moment to this—standing now, staring at him, as he sat in the deep leather chair, one hand raised imperiously to summon her.

It was Xander.

Xander after four years, there again, now visible and in the flesh.

It was as if everything inside her had drained out, leaving her completely, absolutely hollow.

She saw the expression change as in slow-motion across his face. Saw him recognise her.

'Clare?'

She heard him say her name, heard the disbelief in it, even though he was some way from her. Saw him start to his feet, jerk upright.

He started to stride towards her.

She turned and ran.

Blindly she pushed her way across the room, getting to the service door by the bar and thrusting through it. The staff cloakroom was just near, and she dived inside, and then deeper, into the female staff toilet, slamming the door shut and sliding the bolt with fumbling fingers. She yanked down the lid of the toilet and collapsed.

She was shaking. Shaking all over. Shock juddered through her like blows, one after another. How, *how* could Xander have walked in here? Hotels like this, impersonal and anonymous, did not appeal to him. She knew that—that was why she'd taken the risk of getting a job here. If she'd had the slightest idea he'd ever come here she would never have chanced it!

But he had. He had walked in and seen her, and crashed the past right into the present in a single catastrophic moment.

I've got to get out of here!

The need to run overwhelmed her. She had to get out, get home, get away…

Forcibly, she stopped herself shuddering and made herself stand up, walk out into the cloakroom. Her bag and coat were hanging on a peg. The bag held her ordinary clothes, but she didn't waste time changing, only yanking off her high-heeled shoes and slipping her feet into her worn loafers. She could walk faster in them.

Memory sliced through her.

That night, walking out of the St John, walking along the pavements, walking without thought, without direction, without anything in her mind except that terrifying absolute blankness. She did not know how long she had walked. People had bumped her from time to time, or woven past her, and still she had gone on, stopping only at crossings, like a robot, then plunging across when the coast was clear. She had walked and walked.

Eventually, God knew how long later, she'd realised she could not go on, that she was slowing down—as if the last of the battery energy inside her was finally running out. She had looked with blank eyes. She'd been on the far side of Oxford Street, heading towards Marylebone Road, on a street parallel to Baker Street, but much quieter. There had been small hotels there, converted out of the Victorian terraces. There had been one opposite her. It had looked decent enough, anonymous. She'd crossed over the road and gone in.

She had spent the night there, lying in her clothes on the bed, staring blindly up at the ceiling. Very slowly, her mind had started to work. It had been like anaesthesia wearing off.

The agony had been unbearable. Tearing like claws through her flesh. The agony of disbelief, of shock.

Of shame. Shame that she could have been such an incredible fool.

To have been so stupid…

I thought he had started to feel something for me! I thought I meant something to him—had come to be more to him than a mistress…someone who mattered to him. Someone who…

Her hand had slid across her abdomen, and the agony had come again, even more piercing.

What am I going to do?

The words had fallen like stones into her head.

They had gone on falling, heavier and heavier, crushing her, hard and unbearable.

It had taken so long to accept the answer that she had known, with so heavy and broken a heart, was the only one possible.

I did the right thing. I did the only thing.

The words came to her now, as she yanked on her coat.

Nothing else was possible. Nothing.

A hard, steely look came into her eyes. And what did it matter that Xander Anaketos was out there? What did it matter? Nothing at all! He was nothing to her and she—oh, dear God—she was nothing to him.

Had always been nothing to him…

She came back to the present with a jolt. Steeling herself to forget.

Don't remember. Don't think. Just pick up your bag and go. This job is over before it started. I don't care, I'll get another one. Only one thing is important—only one. That I never, ever have to set eyes on Xander Anaketos again.

With grim resolution she walked out of the cloakroom.

He was waiting for her outside.

It was like a blow across her throat, punching the breath from her. Then, with an inhalation that seared in her lungs, she said, 'Let me pass.'

He didn't budge. His frame, large and powerful, blocked the narrow way.

He said something in Greek. She had no idea what it was. It sounded hard, and angry. Then he switched to English.

'What the *hell* did you think you were playing at? Pulling that

disappearing act at the St John when you walked out on me?'
There was naked belligerence in his voice.

Her mouth fell open. Then closed again. A wave of
unreality washed over her, even deeper than the shock waves
that had been washing over her since she'd impacted her eyes
on Xander Anaketos.

'Do you know what hell you put me through?' His tone was
unabated, his dark eyes flashing with dangerous fury.

Sickness warred with shock. She stared at him with wide, un-
comprehending eyes. His dark eyes narrowed.

'I thought you'd been run over, killed, injured. I thought you'd
gone off to someone else. I thought—'

'You thought what?' There was incomprehension as she
spoke. What was he saying? She did not understand.

His eyes flashed again. 'What the hell did you *think* I'd think?
Don't even bother to answer that! It took me a while, but I finally
realised you'd done it entirely on purpose. To get me to come
after you!'

Her mouth fell open. Then closed again. A grim, hard look
came into her face.

'You really thought me that stupid? Stupid enough to think
you'd come chasing after something you'd just replaced with a
new model and paid off with a diamond necklace?'

His expression hardened even more. 'I was concerned about
you,' he bit out.

She laughed. It was a harsh, brief sound. Then it cut out.

'Let me pass,' she said again.

There was a movement behind her, and she turned. Tony, the
barman, had come through the service door, and was regarding
them with a concerned expression.

'Clare—is everything all right? Why have you got your coat on?'
She turned to him.

'Tony—I'm sorry. I'm going home. I can't work here. I apologise for the nuisance. I'll phone Personnel tomorrow and sort out
the formalities.' The words came out staccato and uneven.

He frowned, his eyes going from her to the tall, imposing
figure of someone who very obviously was a guest of the hotel.

'Is there a problem? Do you want me to fetch the manager?' His question embraced both her and Xander Anaketos.

Behind her, Clare heard Xander's voice. The one she was so familiar with. Giving orders to underlings.

'There's no problem,' he said, his accented voice clipped and dismissing. 'I'm seeing Ms Williams home.' He stepped back, giving her room to walk by him. For a moment Clare hesitated, then walked past him. She was not going to make a scene here, in front of Tony. She would get out of the hotel by the service exit, and then head for home. She'd take a taxi. It was an extravagance, but she didn't trust her legs.

It seemed like a million miles to get to the staff entrance, and she could feel Xander's breath almost on her shoulders. She was in shock, she knew. It could not be otherwise. The past had reared up to bite her, like a monstrous creature, and she could not cope with it—could not cope at all…

As she pushed the door open and stepped out on to the pavement by the staff car park, she took in deep, shivering lungfuls of air.

Her elbow was seized in an iron grip.

'This way.'

Her head snapped round, and she pulled away from him violently.

'Let me go!'

'I said, this way,' Xander repeated with grim heaviness.

She tried to shake herself free. It was impossible. His grip was unshakable.

'Do you want me to scream?' she bit out.

'I want you to come this way. You,' he ground out, 'have a lot of explaining to do! I don't appreciate the game you played—'

The word was like a trigger in her skull.

'Game?' She stared at him. Four years had changed him little. It was like looking into the past. The past that had almost destroyed her. The past that was ravening at her again, trying to devour her. Trying to swallow her up with memory of how once her heart had leapt every moment she had seen this man. Each time he had touched her, kissed her, she had come alive…

Pain lashed at her as she stared at him—but what was the use of pain?

It got you nowhere. She'd had four years of knowing that. Four years of getting over it. Moving on. She'd changed.

'Game?' she said again. Her voice was flat now, the emotion gone from her eyes. 'How can you stand there and say that to me? How on earth could you think that I was playing some infantile game? How can you possibly have been anything other than relieved by how I reacted? Do you think I didn't know you by then? Didn't know that you would never tolerate scenes? Let alone by women you had finished with. I saw you when Aimee Decord came up to you, half-cut—remember? That time in Cannes? I saw how ruthless you were to her. So when it was my turn I knew what the score was. You know,' she said, and there was an edge of bitterness in her voice she could not conceal even now, four long years later, 'you should be grateful to me. I must have been the easiest ex-mistress you've ever had.'

Abruptly, he dropped her arm, and stepped back.

'I spent days looking for you! You just vanished.'

His voice was accusatory. His Greek accent thick.

'What are you complaining for?' she flashed back. 'You'd just pressed the delete button on me. I was *supposed* to vanish.'

Xander's expression darkened.

'Do not be absurd! I had made arrangements for you. Of course you were not simply supposed to vanish! Besides, there were all your things still in my apartment—'

Clare's head shook sharply.

'There was nothing of mine there. Nothing personal.'

'There were your clothes, all your belongings!'

'They weren't mine. You'd bought them. Look—what is this? Why this totally pointless post-mortem four years later? You finished with me, and I left. It was very simple. I don't know why you've followed me out here, I don't know why you're talking to me, and I don't know why you think you've got some sort of right to lay into me!'

Her tirade ended, and she could feel her heart pumping like a steam train. Her brain seemed to be whirring like a clock that had suddenly gone from dormant to overwound in ten seconds. She couldn't cope with this—with Xander Anaketos suddenly coming into reality again. It was like some churning hallucinatory dream that she could not believe in.

She turned away, half stumbling. She wanted out. Out, out, *out*. Just at the range of her vision she saw a taxi turn into the concourse of the hotel, towards the main entrance. She ran towards it. If it was depositing someone at the hotel, she could grab it!

A minute later, heart still pounding, she collapsed in the back of the taxi she'd claimed as it pulled out into the busy road again.

She felt sick. Like a concrete mixer on full spin.

It had been Xander—Xander. There, real, alive. Suddenly, out of nowhere, after four years—*four years*—in which her life had changed beyond all recognition.

Her stomach was churning still, shock waves turning her into jelly, her mind a hurricane. The taxi ploughed along the busy arterial road, and headlights flashed into the car. She sat clutching her bag as if it were a lifebelt.

When the cab pulled up outside the house, she fumbled inside the bag for her purse, forcing herself to count out the right money. It was more than she wanted to pay, but she didn't care. She was safe back here again. As she walked up the short path to the front door, getting her key out, she forced herself to be calm. She must not upset Vi.

Oh, God, I've just chucked in my job—I can't tell her that! Not yet.

She opened the door quietly. Vi's bedroom was the front room downstairs, as she found stairs hard to manage these days. The door was half open, and Clare peeped inside. There was Joey, as she'd expected, cosy in a 'nest' on the floor—cushions from the sofa and some extra pillows—snuggled into his child duvet. He was fast asleep and did not stir.

For one long, long moment, Clare stood gazing down at his shadowed form. Her heart turned over, almost stopping.

No! She must not let her thoughts go the way they were about to. She knew what she had been on the point of thinking, and she must not let herself do so. Again, a seismic wave of shock went through her as she fought the acknowledgement of what she had so nearly let come into her mind.

Instead, she backed out. She took off her coat, hung it up on one of the row of pegs beside the stairs, and headed towards the back of the house. There was a small sitting room just in front of the kitchen, and then the bathroom behind the kitchen. Vi was in the kitchen, putting the kettle on for her late-night cup of tea.

'Hello, love,' she said, her voice surprised, as Clare came in. 'You're earlier than you said you would be.'

Clare forced a smile to her face.

'Yes, I thought I'd be later, too,' she said. She left it at that. She could say nothing else. Not right now. Instead, she said, 'How was Joey? He's out like a light now, I see.'

Vi's wrinkled face softened into a familiar smile.

'Oh, he hasn't stirred. Don't you worry about him. Have a nice cup of tea and sit down before you take him upstairs.'

Clare went through into the sitting room and sank down onto the end of the sofa that still had its cushions on. Vi's armchair was closer to the TV in the corner, with a little table beside it, handy for the standard lamp. The room was old-fashioned, like the whole house, but Vi had lived here for thirty years and more.

For Clare it had been a haven. Those first few months, when the life she had been hoping against hope for had simply dissolved in her hands, it had been hideous. But although homeless, at least she had not been destitute. After her father had died she had received an offer for their flat which she'd felt she should not refuse, and she'd put the proceeds into the bank. But she had known she was in no state of mind to sort out her life properly, other than drifting through casual jobs from the temping agency and living in anonymous bedsits, and the money in the bank was still her nest egg. But once she'd known she was going to have to face life as a single mother, she had had to face up to the grim fact that if she bought another flat, even if just a small one, for her to live in, then what would be left for her to live off—and her baby?

The answer had come from a charity supporting single mothers, which put them in touch with elderly people who needed someone to help them continue to live independently in their own homes. So Clare had been introduced to Vi, and Vi had taken to her, and she to the older woman. She had moved into Vi's old-fashioned terraced house in its quiet street in an unexciting but shabbily respectable part of West London. The money in the bank yielded a frugal but sufficient income for everything but luxuries like holidays, and in place of rent she looked after Vi, kept her house for her and kept her company as well, and made her home with her. Now, four years later, Vi was family—an honorary grandmother to Joey, whom she openly adored, and a kind but bracingly realistic support for Clare.

'Here you go, love,' said Vi, making her way slowly into the room, carrying two mugs of tea. Clare took them from her, setting down hers, and putting Vi's on her little table as the old lady sat herself down in her armchair.

'You look peaky,' observed Vi. 'Was it very busy?'

'Yes,' said Clare. She was trying hard to sound normal, look normal. She didn't want Vi upset—not by the fact she'd walked out of her job, nor by something so very much worse.

No—that was forbidden. She was not to think about that. Control. That was the word. The way it had been those first awful months, and then again, when her baby had been put into her arms, and the physical reality of him had brought it piercingly home to her just what she had done.

But it was the right thing to do.

'What you'll need to do, Clare, love,' Vi was saying, 'is give your feet a good soak. Always look after your feet, I say. My gran used to tell me that. She had very bad feet…'

Clare smiled absently, sipping her hot, reviving tea. She let Vi chat on. Vi's mind was as sharp as ever, but she liked to gossip, reminisce, just have someone to talk to. Tonight, though, Clare could hardly focus on what the older woman was telling her. All her energy was being spent on trying to block from her mind what had happened.

I can't think about it now. I'll think about it later. Tomorrow. Next week.

Never…

She had trained herself well not to think of Xander Anaketos. She'd had four long years of doing so.

But conscious thoughts were one thing to control. It was the unconscious ones she dreaded. And that night, as she lay in her bed upstairs, Joey in the little room beside her, asleep in his own bed now, as it had always been, her dreams that betrayed her.

Dreams of Xander, his strong body arching over hers, his mouth on hers, his hands on her breasts, her flanks, stroking and smoothing, gliding and arousing, so arousing, taking her onwards, ever onwards, to that wonderful, ecstatic place where he had always taken her…always.

She awoke in the early hours, sick and heart pounding. The dreams had been so real, so vivid, with the horrible, super-realistic feelings that only dreams could have. Her stomach writhed, her pulse racing like a panic attack.

And her breasts, she realised with a sick horror, were swollen, her nipples distended.

She jerked out of bed, padding with bare feet down the stairs to the bathroom, feeling sick and ashamed.

The day passed with agonising slowness. She seemed to be two people. The person she always was these days—Joey's doting mother, attentive to him, responsive to him, adoring of him, and Vi's companion, bringing breakfast to her before she made her slow morning toilette, and then, after lunch, making their familiar daily expedition to the nearby park, Vi walking slowly with her stick and Clare pushing Joey in his buggy. In the park, Vi sat on her usual seat, and Joey got stuck in with Clare. First to the sandpit and then the playground, and the expedition ended with the usual ritual of taking Joey to feed the ducks on the pond. All blessedly familiar.

But she was someone else as well, she knew. Someone who was still jarring with shock, with disbelief that she had actually seen Xander Anaketos again, spoken to him, run from him…

He's gone. It's over.

She kept telling herself that repeatedly, as the other person she was went through the familiar rituals in the park.

I've got to calm down. I've got to get back to normal. I've got to forget it happened.

But it seemed so cruel. It had been such agony four years ago, to do what she had known she must—get over it, move on—but she had done it. She'd had to put her son first. And they were safe now. Secure. Familiar.

The past was gone.

Last night had been nothing but an aberration. And she had run from it, just as she had run from that hideous night when her stupid, stupid hopes and illusions had been ripped from her.

'Let's go, Mummy!' Joey's little voice was a welcome interruption from her tormenting thoughts. He lifted up the empty plastic bag that had contained the bread crusts. 'All gone,' he announced.

'Time for tea,' said Vi, and got slowly to her feet from the bench she'd been sitting on.

Then they headed homewards in a slow procession.

She had no premonition. No warning. Just as she had had none last night.

As they rounded the corner into the street where Vi's house was it was Joey who spoke first, pointing.

'Big car!'

Clare followed the direction of his pointing, and slowly her heart stopped in her chest. Outside Vi's house was parked a long, lean, brilliant scarlet monster of a car.

And out of it Xander Anaketos was emerging.

Why? That was the first weird thought in Clare's stricken brain. Why was he here? What for? What else could he possibly have to say to her, now he'd vented his spleen at her for daring not to be disposed of in exactly the way he liked to get rid of discarded mistresses?

Then, like an explosion in slow motion, she realised that it didn't matter why he had come here, or how he had found out where she lived.

Because as he started to walk towards them she realised he was not looking at her. His eyes were entirely, terrifyingly, on Joey.

Her breath was crushed from her lungs. She gave a silent, inaudible, breathless scream inside her head.

Desperately her brain worked feverishly. If she could just

bundle Joey inside, without him getting close enough to make out his features…

But it was too late. She could see it. See it in the change of expression in Xander's face. See the shock—the disbelief—jagging across his features.

He stopped. Just halted where he was, in the middle of the pavement, some yards from them.

Greek came from him. Hollow. Rasping.

Then slowly, very slowly, his eyes lifted from his son and went to her.

There was murder in his face.

CHAPTER THREE

XANDER got them indoors. He had no memory of how he'd done it, or of what house they'd gone into. No awareness of anything other than the raw, boiling rage thundering through him. His mind had gone into a white-out.

Somehow, and he had no conscious thought of how, he had got her away from the old woman and the boy.

My son. Theos—*my son!*

There was no doubt about it—could not be! He could see his own features in the child's face.

And in hers—oh, he could see completely, absolutely, that she knew the toddler she was pushing along was his. She'd given birth to *his* son!

An iron will clamped down over the raging voice in his head. Control. That was what he needed now—absolute, total control. He was good at control. He had practised it all his life, from childhood with his stern uncle, who had required silence while he worked, and carrying the same discipline into his business dealings—never letting his rivals see his hand, always concealing his thoughts and aims from them.

And control, too, had been his watchword when it came to his dealings with women. It was the reason he changed them so frequently. A rule he had bent only once…

The irony of it savaged him.

Emotion surged in him like a terrifying monster, but he slammed it back down as he marched Clare down through the house, out through a door at the back, yanking it open and thrusting her outside. There was a garden there, narrow and quite long, with a plastic sand tray and a miniature slide. There were children's toys, a ball, a push-along dog and some big colourful bricks, on the small stone-paved patio before the lawn started.

He grabbed her elbows and hauled her round.

'Talk,' he said.

His eyes bored down into hers like drills.

Her face had gone white. He was not surprised. Guilt was blazoned across it. Rage spurted through him again. The vicious, vengeful bitch! To keep his son from him! Deliberately, knowingly…

'Talk!' he snarled again.

Her face seemed to work, but not well. Slowly, faintly, she spoke.

'What do you want me to say? There's nothing *to* say.'

He shook her like a rag, and she was boneless in his grip.

'You keep my son from me and say there's nothing to say?' he demanded, fury icing through his words, his features. 'Just what kind of a vengeful *bitch* are you?'

Her expression changed. Blanked.

'What?' she said. There was complete incomprehension in her voice.

He shook her again. Emotion was ravening in him, like a wolf.

'To keep my son from me as some kind of sick revenge!'

Her mouth opened, then closed. Then suddenly she tore free.

'What the *hell* do you think you're saying to me?'

His eyes darkened like night.

'You kept my son from me because you were angry that I finished with you!'

Her face worked again, but this time there was a different emotion in it. Her features contorted.

'You conceited oaf!' she gasped at him. 'Just who do you think you are? First you think I played some stupid manipulative game by walking out the way I did! Now you think, you *really* think, that I didn't tell you I was pregnant so I could get some kind of *revenge* on you?'

'What other reason can there be?' he snarled back at her.

A choking sound came from her.

'How about the fact you'd just replaced me with a new model and had given me my pay-off of a diamond necklace, like I was some kind of *whore*?' she spat at him.

Xander's mouth whitened.

'You knew you were pregnant that evening?' His voice was a raw rasp. 'You knew you were pregnant and you kept *quiet* about it! You walk out, carrying my baby, and you never say a *word* to me—in *four years*?'

She was staring at him. Staring at him as if he had spoken in Greek.

'Well?' he demanded. His jaw was gritted, fury still roiling inside him. Fury and another emotion, even more powerful, that he must not, must *not* yet yield to, but which was driving him—driving him onwards with impossible motion.

'You're not real,' she said. Her voice had changed. 'You're just not real. You actually think I would tell a man who'd chucked me on the garbage pile, who'd paid me off with a diamond necklace, that I was pregnant by him?'

His expression stiffened. 'I did not "pay you off",' he bit out. 'It's customary to give a token of appreciation to—'

'Don't say that word to me! Don't *ever* say that word to me again! And don't even think of trying to tell me that after you'd just flushed me down the pan I was supposed to announce I was carrying your child.'

Emotion was mounting in Xander's chest.

'If you had told me, obviously I would have rescinded my decision to—'

A look of incredulity passed across her contorted features.

'Rescinded your decision?' Her voice was high-pitched and hollow. 'It wasn't a bloody business meeting. You had made it clear—absolutely, killingly clear—that I was out. You had someone new to warm your bed and that was that.'

His face tightened. 'Obviously, had you told me that you had got pregnant, then everything would have been very different.'

She turned away. The gesture angered him. He reached out for her again, his hand closing on her shoulder.

She froze at his touch. He could feel it, all her muscles tensing. Her reaction angered him even more. Why should she resist him?

She never resisted me—always yielded to me…eager for me. All that cool, English composure dissolved, like ice in heat…my heat…

He thrust the memory aside. It was irrelevant. All that was relevant now was to deal with this shattering discovery.

I have a son!

The impulse, overwhelming and overpowering, to go now, this instant, to find the child that was inside the house, find him and—

No, he could not do that either. Not yet. Not until—until… *Christos*, he could hardly think straight, his mind a storm of emotion.

His hand dropped from her.

'As,' he said heavily, 'it will be different now.'

She was still half turned away from him. He could not see her face. He didn't care. Providing she could hear, could understand, that was all that mattered. He fought the storm inside him for control. He had been iron-willed all day. Controlled enough to instruct his London PA, very calmly, to find out the address of Clare Williams from the hotel she had been working at. Detached enough to rearrange today's schedule so that he could be free by late afternoon to drive and find her. She'd run out on him once before, vanished into the night—she was not going to do so a second time.

But the reason he had sought her out had evaporated—instantly, like water in a volcano—the moment he had realised just what Clare Williams had done to him…

Emotion whipped through him again, that white-hot disbelieving fury that had ripped through him the moment his eyes had gone to the child in the buggy she had been pushing.

That was all that concerned him. *That* was all that consumed him.

But he must control it. Giving vent to the storm inside him would achieve nothing. With Herculean effort, he hammered down his emotions.

'I want to see him.'

His voice was flat. Very controlled.

She turned her head back towards him. Her eyes were quite blank.

She uttered a single word. A word that went into him like a knife.

'Why?' she said.

Carefully, very carefully, he layered icy control over his features.

'Because he is my son,' he enunciated. Then, before she could answer, he walked back indoors.

The elderly woman was in the small, drab sitting room. It looked ancient, and so did she. She was sitting in an armchair and the television was on, with a cartoon. His son was sitting on her lap, lolled back on her, all his attention on the screen.

As Xander walked in, the woman looked at him. She was old, but her eyes were sharp. They rested on him for a second, then went past him. Behind him, Xander could sense Clare. The child did not look round.

The knife went into Xander again. He did not know the name of his own son.

'Tell me his name.'

He spoke quietly, but there was an insistence in it that would not be brooked. It was the old woman who answered.

'It's Joey,' she said. 'Joey, pet—say hello.'

Reluctantly, the toddler twisted his head briefly. ''Lo,' he said, then went straight back to the cartoon.

He must be gone three, Xander thought. I have a three-year-old son, and I never knew. I never knew…

The storm of emotion swirled up in him again, but he forced it back. The elderly woman was looking at him. She had a steady gaze. Did she realise who he was? He assumed so. He had recognised his son instantly. It would not be hard to see him in Joey, and know that he must be the boy's father.

His throat convulsed, and again he had to take a deep, steadying breath. He opened his mouth to speak, but the old woman was before him.

'Clare, love, Joey needs his tea. The programme will be over soon, and he'll realise he's hungry. I'd do something quick for him, if I were you. Eggy soldiers is always nice, isn't it?'

She spoke cheerfully, calmly, as if she were not witnessing a man discovering his three-year-old son.

She was right to do so, Xander realised. Whatever else, his son—

Joey—must not be upset. What must be settled now would not be helped by his giving voice to fury, his emotions. Abruptly, he sat himself down on the rather battered sofa, opposite his son. He said nothing, just watched him watching the television with a rapt expression on his face, interrupted by bursts of childish laughter.

My son!

The storm of emotion in Xander's breast swirled, then gradually, very gradually subsided. But deep inside his heart seemed to swell and swell.

Clare put the eggs to boil. She got out the bread, and popped it in the toaster. She fetched some milk, and poured it into Joey's drinking cup. She set out a tray with his plastic plate with pictures of puppies on it, and started to pare an apple for his pudding. She worked swiftly, mindlessly.

She mustn't think about this. Mustn't do anything. Just give Joey his tea.

When it was ready she carried it through. The programme's credits were rolling, and Joey had returned to the real world. He looked about him.

'Time for tea,' he announced. Then he focussed on the man looking at him. 'Hello,' he said. He looked interestedly at the man who had started his life four long years ago.

Xander looked at the child who was his. Emotion felled him. For a moment his brain went completely and absolutely blank. What did he know of children? His own childhood was so far away that he never thought of it—his father had been dead, his mother too. He had no memories of them.

Cold iced in his spine. If he had not come today, sought out the woman who had walked out into the night four years ago, his own son would, like him, have had no memories of his father…

That will not be…

Resolution steeled inside him. His son would have a father, and memories of a father, starting right now.

'Hello, Joey,' said Xander. 'I am your father. I've come to see you.'

Clare felt the knife go through her throat, and she gasped

aloud. Xander ignored her. So did Joey. Joey tilted his head and subjected Xander to an intense look.

'Fathers are daddies,' he announced.

Xander nodded. 'Quite right. You're a clever boy.'

Joey looked pleased with himself.

'Clare, give Joey his tea. He's a growing boy.' Vi beckoned to her, and cleared some space on the table by her chair. Shakily, Clare crossed and put down the tray.

'Soldiers!' shouted Joey, pleased. 'Eggy soldiers.' He seized one of the fingers of toast and plunged it into one of the two eggs with the end sliced off, starting to eat with relish. Around his neck, Vi was deftly attaching a bib.

It was all, thought Clare, with a sick, hollow feeling inside her, intensely normal.

Except for one thing.

She rubbed a hand over her brow, her eyes going to the man sitting on Vi's old sofa. The man who was her son's father. This couldn't be happening. It just couldn't. Wave after wave of disbelief was eddying through her. So much shock. Last night had been bad enough, but now this… This was a nightmare. She couldn't think, couldn't feel. Could only watch, with a strange unnatural calm, how Xander Anaketos was watching his son—her son—eat his tea.

He stayed for another half an hour. Time for Joey to finish his tea and start playing with his toys. Clare washed up, trying to do anything to bring back normality—to pretend that her life hadn't just crashed all around her. She started to get her and Vi's supper ready, taking a cup of tea in to the other woman. Silently, she placed a mug of instant coffee—black, as she knew he liked his coffee—beside Xander. He gave her a long, level look that was quite expressionless. Then he returned his attention to his son, asking him about the car he was pushing around on the carpet.

'I like cars,' said Joey.

'So do I,' she heard Xander say. 'When you're bigger you can ride in my car.'

'The big red one?' asked Joey interestedly.

'Yes, that one.'

'Does it go fast?' Joey enquired, making 'vrooming' noises with his own toy car.

'Very fast,' said Xander.

'I like fast,' said Joey.

'Me too,' agreed his father.

'Can we see it now, outside?'

'Next time. Today it's too late,'

'All right. Next time.' Joey was contented. He went on chatting to his father.

All the while Vi sat and did her knitting, the needles clicking away rhythmically.

Xander did not speak to Clare until just before he left.

'I must go now, Joey,' he said. 'But I'll come back tomorrow.'

'OK,' said Joey. 'Then I'll see your car. Bye.'

Xander looked down at him, one long last look, drinking in every detail, then turned to go. Clare followed him down the narrow hallway to the front door. As he opened it he turned to her.

'If you try and run again,' he said, and the way he spoke made the hairs rise on the back of her neck, 'I will hunt you down. Tomorrow—' he looked at her, his eyes like weights, pressing into her '—we talk.'

Then he was gone.

'Vi—what am I going to do? What am I going to do?' Clare's voice was anguished. Upstairs, Joey slept peacefully, though it had taken him longer to go down than usual. He'd started talking about 'the man who said he was my father'. It was more curiosity, Clare thought, than reality. But she had been as evasive as she could without arousing suspicion.

A spurt of anger went through her—another one. They'd been coming and going with vicious ferocity ever since she'd shut the door on Xander.

How *could* he have said that to Joey? Right out—bald. Undeniable. Unqualifiable!

At just gone three, Joey was still feeling his way in using language, and Clare was never entirely sure how much he understood, how much he took in.

Now she sat, her hands wringing together, gazing hopelessly across at Vi.

For a moment Vi did not reply, concentrating on a tricky bit in her knitting. Then, without looking up, she said, 'You know, Clare, love, I've never been one to give advice when it's not asked for. But…' her old shrewd eyes glanced at the younger woman '…whatever you do, it has to be what's best for Joey. Not for you. I know that's hard. I know you came here to me when you were very unhappy, and I know you told me that Joey's dad wasn't ever going to be someone who would care about him or you, that he'd just pay money and nothing more, and wish Joey to perdition, and that wouldn't be good for any child. But—' her voice changed a little, taking on the very slightest reproving note, while still staying sympathetic '—that man doesn't seem like the one you told me about when you came here. That's an angry man, love—and not because he's found out about having a son. If he was angry for that reason, why did he stay here and tell Joey he was his dad? He wants to *be* Joey's dad, that's what.'

Clare just stared. 'Vi, you don't understand. He's not an ordinary man—he isn't a "dad" as you call it! He lives a life you can't imagine—'

She fell silent. In her mind she felt time collapse, and saw again the gilded, expensive world that Xander Anaketos moved in—where she had once moved at his side, gowned in dresses costing thousands of pounds, jewels even more—a world as unreal to her now, when her horizons were bounded by finding the best bargains in supermarkets, by ceaseless careful budgeting and never splashing out on anything, as if he came from a different planet.

Vi shook her head. 'If he wants to be Joey's dad you can't stop him, love.'

Clare's expression hardened. 'The fathers of illegitimate children in this country have no legal rights over them,' she exclaimed harshly.

Vi gave her a long look over her knitting needles.

'We're not talking law and rights—we're talking about being a dad to a little lad.'

'I won't have Joey hurt.' Clare's voice was passionate. 'I won't have him thinking he's got a father, and then he hasn't. I won't have Xander swanning in here, upsetting him! Joey's got *me*!'

Vi put her knitting down. 'Oh, love,' she said, her voice sorrowful. 'He'll always have you. But you can't stop him from knowing his dad—it wouldn't be right.'

'But *why* does Xander care about Joey? He *doesn't* care. That's the *point*! Vi—you don't know him. He's not a man who can feel for others—I know that. Dear God, I know that. He's just angry because… Because…'

She felt silent again, her chest painful. *Why* was he so angry? She didn't understand—she just didn't. Xander hadn't wanted her, had thrown her out like last year's model, chucked and discarded, paid off with a diamond necklace. So why, *why* had it angered him that she'd disappeared just as he had *wanted* her to?

Anger warred with anguish.

Vi sighed. A long, heavy sigh, from one who had seen a lot of sorrows in life and knew there wasn't always anything that could be done about them.

'Why not just see what happens, pet?' she said. 'You'll always do what's best for Joey. You always have, you always will.'

The hard, painful knot in Clare's breast eased, just a fraction. But she still looked at Vi with fear in her eyes. Her heart was squeezed tight, as if in a vice, painful and crushed. Emotion was inside her like a huge, swelling balloon, filling her up, terrifying her. How, *how* could it be that a bare twenty-four hours ago her life had been normal…safe? Her stomach churned again—it had been doing that over and over, making her feel sick and disbelieving. Hadn't it been bad enough setting eyes on Xander again like that last night, having the past leap out of nowhere and slam her into the ground like that?

But that had been nothing to what she had gone through— was still going through—when he had found out about Joey.

The sick feeling intensified. Oh, dear God, what was she going to do?

And even more frightening, more unthinkable, what was Xander Anaketos going to do now that he knew he had a son…?

CHAPTER FOUR

XANDER stood at the window of the reception room in his London apartment, the morning sunshine streaming in. There were no memories of Clare here. He'd moved on since then, and this apartment must be the second or even third he occupied when he was in the UK on business. It was the same with his places in Paris, New York, Rome and Athens. He didn't keep things long. He changed his cars every year or so, whenever a new model of his favourite marque came out. He changed his watches just as often, whenever a newer and better one was launched. Similarly the yachts he kept at Piraeus and the South of France.

He had no sentimental attachments to things.

Or to women. He changed those just as frequently. He always had. There was, after all, no reason not to...

But a child—a child could not be changed. A child was for ever.

Emotion knifed through him. It had been doing so regularly for the last thirty-six hours. Ever since he'd looked up in the cocktail lounge and seen, for the first time in four years, the woman who had got up from the table at the St John with a low murmur and walked out, vanishing into the night.

He saw again her blank, expressionless eyes as he told her, 'It's over.'

Christos—she was already pregnant. She sat there, carrying my son, and then walked out on me without a word. Taking my son with her.

Fury bit savagely. He turned abruptly away from the window and headed for the door. It was time to get this sorted. Time to get his son.

Tension racked through Clare like wire stringing her from the ceiling. She was standing rigid as a board in her bedroom, the upstairs room above Vi's bedroom, because it was the only place they could be without Joey hearing them from the back sitting room, where he was with Vi, while opposite her Xander stood, his back to the window, silhouetted against the light. It made him look very tall and dark.

Clare felt again that sickening sense of unreality sweep over her.

And something else, too. Something that had nothing to do with the hideous fact that Xander had discovered Joey's existence and everything to do with the way she was so stupidly, insanely aware of his devastating effect on her.

As she had always been…

No! Dear God, out of everything in this nightmare that was the last, the very last thing she must think about. Once, so fatally, she had been vulnerable to the man who stood looking grimly at her now. But that had been a lifetime ago. Once, so pathetically, she had thought she might mean something to him. But in one callous utterance he had ripped that pathetic hope from her…

He had started to speak, his voice harsh and clipped, his accent even more pronounced than usual. Clare forced herself to listen, however much her stomach was churning.

'My lawyers are making the necessary arrangements,' Xander was announcing. 'There will need to be a prenuptial agreement, and for that reason the ceremony itself must be on a territory where it is legally binding—which is not, so I am informed, the case in the UK. Is, therefore, your passport up to date? And does my son have one of his own? If not, this will need to be expedited. You will also—'

'What are you talking about?' Clare's voice was blank, cutting across his.

'I am telling you what will need to be done for us to marry—

quickly,' Xander said. His mouth tightened automatically at her interruption—and her question.

'*What?*' Incomprehension, disbelief yawned through her.

His eyes flashed darkly. 'Did you not realise that I would be prepared to marry you?'

Clare shook her head. 'No.'

Her voice was hollow.

Xander looked down at her. Had she really not thought he would do so? His gaze narrowed. Was that why she had walked out on him that night four years ago? Had she not realised that he would marry her?

Of course he would have married a woman carrying his child. Especially—

No. He slammed down the lid on the memory. That was then, this was now.

'I would have married you four years ago if you had taken the trouble to tell me you were carrying my child,' he said tersely.

'Would you?' Clare replied slowly. 'Would you really?'

'Of course.' His voice was stiff.

For one terrible moment pain ripped through Clare. Oh, God, if she had taken that other road—the one she had refused to take, the one she had had to find all the strength she possessed not to take, not to go back to him, to seek him out, to risk telling him she was pregnant…to risk him rejecting her unborn child.

But she had assumed that he would never in a million years have thought to marry her. She would have been given an allowance, a gagging order so she could not babble to the press about any 'love-child' of Xander Anaketos, and then dumped in some expensive villa somewhere where she could raise her son as the unwanted bastard of a discarded mistress…

He would have married me!

Pain ripped again.

Agony.

Because that was what it would have been—just as much as if she had been kept as his discarded mistress bearing his bastard. The agony of being married to him for no reason other than that she had conceived his child. When all along she would have known—as she knew now, so bitterly, had known since that last, lacerating evening with him—just how *nothing* she was to him.

She looked at him now. Just as he had been able four years ago to stop the breath in her lungs, so he could still do now. The passage of four years had merely matured his features. The breathtaking impact of his masculinity still was as potent as ever.

It would have been torment to have been married to him. And there could still be no greater torment…

'So,' he continued, his voice still clipped and harsh, 'now that you have understood that, perhaps we can finally proceed? If you pack promptly, we can be at my apartment for lunch. Please ensure you have all the legal documents required, such as my son's birth certificate, and—'

'I'm not going to marry you!' Clare's voice rang out.

'You will,' he commanded.

She took a step backwards. She could not be hearing this. She could not be hearing Xander Anaketos calmly announcing that she would marry him. Was he mad?

'Do not play games over this,' Xander bit back angrily. 'Of course we shall marry.'

She shook her head violently. 'It's insane to think so!'

Xander's eyes darkened. 'If it is the prenuptial agreement you object to—tough. That is not negotiable. You've hardly proved trustworthy'

She gave a laugh. It had a note of hysteria in it. It made Xander's eyes focus on her even more narrowly. She rubbed a hand over her brow.

'This is insane,' she said heavily. 'It's mad that you should even think of marrying me like this.' She lifted her eyes to him. 'I never wanted you to know about Joey. Never!' She saw his eyes darken malevolently at her words, but ploughed on, ignoring his reaction. 'I wish you had never found out,' she said bleakly. 'I wish I had never set eyes on you again. But it's too late now. Too late.' Her voice was heavy. Then she looked at him, her shoulders squaring. 'I won't marry you—it's insane even to think it!'

Something moved in his eyes. Something that made her feel

faint. Then there was a caustic etching of lines around his mouth as he replied.

'You are saying you prefer *this*—' he gestured with his hand, his eyes sweeping the room, which was furnished with old-fashioned furniture from Vi's younger days, worn now, as were the carpet and the curtains '—to the life you would lead as my wife?'

'Yes,' said Clare. 'If all I cared about was your money, Xander, don't you think I'd have told you I was pregnant—even if you had just thrown me out like garbage?'

His eyes flashed again. 'I did not "throw you out like garbage"! I made suitable alternative arrangements for your accommodation. I gave you a suitable token of my apprec—'

'*Don't say that word!* If you say it *one* more time to me, I swear to God I will…I will…'

She sat down heavily on the bed, and the springs creaked. Her legs would not hold her up any more.

She looked across at him. He was standing stiffly, rigid.

'Oh, go to hell,' she mumbled. 'Just go to hell, Xander. I know the law will let you have some visiting rights to Joey, and if you really insist on them I know I can't stop you. But don't *ever* think you're going to get any more. I don't want you in my life again.'

His face stilled. It sent a shiver of foreboding through her.

'But I,' he said, 'have every intention of being in my son's life. I have every intention of being his father.'

She gave a twisted laugh, cut short.

'Father? You don't know the slightest thing about being a father.'

For a moment there was a silence that could have been cut with a knife.

'Thanks to you,' said Xander, softly and sibilantly. 'Because of you, I am a stranger to my own son. I did not even know his *name* when I spoke to him!'

Clare's mouth tightened. She would not let him make her feel guilty. She would not. She stood up, forcing herself upright, folding her arms tightly across her chest. Her chin lifted.

'Well, if you're so keen to be a father, come and learn to be one. But listen to me—and listen to me well!' Her expression grew fierce. 'Fatherhood is for *life,* Xander! It's not some novelty that you can amuse yourself with or get off on self-righteously because I dared to object to the way you treated me and never told you about Joey. Don't think that being stinking rich means you can just have the easy bits and dump the rest on your paid minions! And above all—' she bit each word out '—it is *not* something you do without committing to it for the rest of your life. Because if you hurt my son—if you cause a single tear to fall from his eyes because you get bored with him, or put yourself first, or put making money first or, God help you, play with your mistresses first!—then you won't be *fit* to be his father!'

She could see anger light in his face, but she didn't care. Didn't give a toss! She glared at him, and he met her eyes with his dark, heavy ones. Then, abruptly, she spoke again.

'I can't cope. I can't cope with this. It's like a steam train going over me. The day before yesterday everything was normal. Now it's—' She closed her eyes. 'A nightmare.'

'A nightmare?' Xander echoed her words. His voice was cold and vicious.

'Yes!' Her eyes flared open again. 'I never wanted to see you again. Not for the rest of my life. But you're here—and it's a nightmare. And I can't cope with it. I just can't. I just *can't*…' She took a deep, shuddering intake of breath. 'Look—I need time…time to get used to this. I've been in shock since that night at the hotel—and I don't handle shock well. I can't get my head round it.'

'You want my *sympathy*?' Xander's voice was incredulous.

'I don't want *anything* from you!' she bit back. 'Like I said, I wish to God I'd never set eyes on you again. But it's too late. So I'm simply telling you how it is for me—too much to handle right now. And you know something?' Her eyes flashed again. 'I don't *have* to handle it right now. I don't have to do anything until you come back here with a court order for access in your hand. Right now, if I wanted to, I could phone the police and tell them you're an intruder here. So back off, Xander. Back off and give me the time I need to get my head round this.'

'The time you need to run, perhaps? The way you like to do?' His voice was silky and dangerous.

Her face tightened. 'I won't run, Xander. That would be playing into your hands, wouldn't it? And besides—where would I go? I can't leave Vi.'

He frowned.

'You can pay rent elsewhere, not just to your current landlady.'

'Vi isn't my landlady. She's my friend. And she doesn't charge rent because I help look after her so she can go on living here, in her own home. She's like a grandmother to Joey. Family. I could never leave her!'

She dropped her arms to her sides, weariness and defeat filling her. 'Look, I can't take any more right now. I want you to go. I won't run—I can't. If you don't believe me, set some guards or whatever round the house to make sure I don't. I don't care. But just go. Say goodbye to Joey if you want.'

'That is very generous of you.' His sarcasm was open, and Clare felt herself flushing. Then her face hardened again.

'Joey needs to take this slowly too, Xander. He needs to get used to you. And most of all—' her eyes were like needles '—he needs not to depend on you to stay interested in him.'

For a moment she thought she could see murder in the dark, long-lashed eyes that had once, so long ago, melted her bones.

'I don't have to prove myself to you,' he said, with a softness that raised the hair on the back of her neck. 'Only to my son.'

Then he turned and walked out of the room, down the stairs. His tread was heavy on the floorboards. Like hammers going into her chest.

She stayed upstairs in her room, standing motionless, as if wire was wrapping her round, biting into her cruelly. It seemed for ever until she heard his tread on the hall carpet and the sound of the front door opening, then closing.

Slowly, she went downstairs again.

Joey was taking one of his picture books across to Vi, but as Clare came in he looked round.

'That was my daddy here,' he announced. 'There's a daddy in this book. Look.'

He opened the book to a page showing a happy nuclear family, sitting having a meal around a table, with a baby and a toddler.

It wasn't a book Clare liked—because of the nuclear family—but Joey had chosen it because it included a scene where the toddler was playing with a very impressive toy garage.

His stubby finger pointed at each person in the illustration.

'Mummy, Daddy, me.' Then he frowned. 'Baby,' he said. He looked at Clare. 'We haven't got a baby.'

Clare swallowed. 'No, but we've got a nan instead. That's a different family from us, Joey.'

Joey looked at her. 'Can we keep my daddy?' he asked.

Clare could see Vi's eyes on her. Eyes that said nothing—and knew everything. She crouched down beside Joey.

'Your daddy doesn't live in this country, darling. He travels all over the world. Lots of countries. So you won't see him very often.'

Joey's eyes clouded.

'He said he was coming back. When?'

'Soon,' said Clare. She got to her feet.

Too soon.

Her stomach churned at the thought.

Xander gave her till the weekend. He used the time to his own advantage. In a series of punishing meetings, and flights to Geneva, Milan and Paris, he got through of a formidable amount of work.

He also disposed of Sonja de Lisle. She was no longer a requirement, only an unnecessary complication.

When he gave her the news, she flew into a tantrum. Eyes spitting, language foul, she stormed out, with her suitcases filled to bursting with every garment, accessory and piece of jewellery he'd ever bought her.

Four hours later she was back on the phone to him, purring away and saying it had all been a mistake on her part, enticing him back to her, inviting him over to a very intimate dinner in the suite at the Grosvenor he'd taken for her, to ease her departure.

He hung up on her in mid-purr.

Memory sliced through him like a meat cleaver—to the time when he'd got rid of another woman from his life.

Those expressionless eyes, that very still face…

Now he knew why. She'd already known she was pregnant,

and when he'd called time on her she'd decided that her revenge on him would be to keep his child from her. And she was doing the same thing in refusing to marry him. Keeping him at arm's length from his son. Anger bit in him like a scorpion's sting. And she'd had the unmitigated gall to claim it was because he was inexperienced with children—

Her doing. She kept my son from me, and now accuses me of knowing nothing about him.

Rage boiled in him. Then he quenched it. He would get his son. Joey would grow up with him. There was no question—no question whatsoever. Whatever it took to achieve that, he would do.

He picked up the phone on his desk and summoned his PA. His instructions to her had nothing to do with business…

CHAPTER FIVE

'WELL,' announced Vi robustly, 'to my mind it's just the thing to get little Joey used to you.'

Her eyes went approvingly to Xander. Clare, at the furthest end possible of the sofa, stared aghast at Vi.

'You can't mean that!'

How could Vi be taking Xander's part? How could she even be civil to him? She was being even more than civil—she was treating him with approbation. She'd all but forced Clare to take Joey out to the park with Xander today, when he'd turned up just after lunchtime on the first day of the weekend. Clare had walked in stony silence, pushing the buggy, while Xander focussed all his attention on Joey. It had been excruciating.

His arrival back at Vi's house after four days had sent her hopes plummeting. She'd been hoping against hope that he'd gone abroad, summoned by all his complex international business dealings. Yet even the few days' intermission had allowed her, she knew, to mitigate the demolishing shock that had possessed her. She'd had time to accept that the nightmare was real, that Xander Anaketos had found out about Joey—and that he wanted to be a part of Joey's life.

And Joey, it seemed, twisting the knife in her breast, was of the same opinion. His childish conversation had returned to the subject of his father time and again over the last few days, and even though Clare had done her best to change the subject, Vi, of all people, had been matter-of-fact in answering.

'He'll come when he can, lamb. Dads have to work, remember? So he's very busy.'

But not busy enough. Clare had heard his monster of a car arrive as Joey was finishing his lunch, and her heart had sunk to her shoes. Now it had congealed into cold ice. Was he insane, thinking she and Joey would go on *holiday* with him? Yet here was Vi, thinking it was a perfectly unexceptional thing to suggest.

'Yes,' Vi retorted. 'A holiday together would be just the thing. It's a very good idea.'

'I don't *want* to!' Clare exclaimed vehemently.

Vi gave her a level look. 'Joey's got a right to his father, love,' she said calmly. Her gaze went to Xander again. He gave her a slight nod of acknowledgement.

Clare was staring at Vi as if she were a traitor.

'He can come and visit *here*!' she countered.

'Well, he will, love. And he is already, and that's all very well. But Joey needs to spend more time than just an outing to the park or some playtime indoors. A holiday would be just the thing, like I say.'

'I couldn't possibly leave you, Vi. How would you manage?' Clare said desperately.

'That has been taken care of,' Xander interjected. 'Mrs Porter has been good enough to accept a minute token of my appreciation for her contribution to the care of my son over these last years. While Joey is on holiday she will be too.'

'That's right,' said Vi. 'Though I don't need thanking—Clare and Joey are family to me. But I'll be very glad to see Devon again.'

Clare felt another punch of betrayal go throughher. 'We were going to go there all together! In the summer—'

'Well, Clare, love, a caravan always was going to be a bit tricky for me, wasn't it? And this hotel I'm going to is specially adapted for old people, and it's right on the sea front. It couldn't be better. And this time of year the town won't be too crowded either—nor the weather too hot for me.'

'So, do you have any more objections?'

Clare's eyes snapped to those of the figure at the other end of the sofa. Somewhere deep inside, on a different plane of exis-

tence from the one her mind was occupying, something deto-
nated. Xander was not wearing a business suit today. He wore
the kind of casual wear that looked relaxed but was, she could
tell at a glance, extremely expensive. His dark blue sweater was
cashmere, his loafers hand-made, his petrol-blue trousers
bespoke tailored.

But it wasn't his clothes that had caused the detonation.

It was the body beneath…

The body she had once known with such sensual intimacy that
if she even began to remember it would crucify her…

I don't need this.

Wasn't it hideous enough having to watch Xander with
Joey—and, worse, Joey responding with increasing confidence
and pleasure to all the attention from him? Wasn't that enough
torment for her?

Why did her own self have to betray her as well?

There was only one cruel comfort, if such a thing were
possible in this nightmare that had engulfed her since she had
come face to face with Xander Anaketos again. Only one.

That, whatever her treacherous memory might be trying to
conjure back, it was finding no answering echo within him.

From him came only grim hostility and condemnation.

*Be grateful for it, she thought. Be grateful he treats you like
a block of wood!*

And she must do likewise. It was the only way she would be
able to cope.

But how could she possibly survive a holiday in his company?
She couldn't. It was impossible.

'Well?' Xander's prompt came again. 'Do you think Joey
would not enjoy the seaside?'

She would not, *would not* be steamrollered like this.

'He can enjoy it here, in this country. Taking him to the
Caribbean is just ridiculous.'

'It's at its best at this time of year,' said Xander. 'And though
the flight is long, one of the advantages of a private plane is that
we can not only fly whenever we want, but there will be ample
room for Joey to move about freely and be entertained. Surely

you remember,' he said, and his eyes levelled at her, 'how easy travel is when you can do it in comfort?'

She pulled her eyes away. Oh, God, she remembered only too well. Remembered how Xander had taken advantage of the sleeping accommodation on his private long-haul jet.

Not that that they had slept much…

'Joey will have a lovely time,' Vi said, speaking decisively. 'And that's what's important. Isn't it, Clare, love?'

She looked speakingly across at her, and all Clare could do was feel totally, absolutely betrayed.

Xander got to his feet. 'My PA will be in touch on Monday, and will make all the arrangements necessary—including whatever is needed to expedite Joey's passport.' He glanced at his watch.

The gesture was not lost on Clare. It was Saturday—Xander Anaketos would not be spending the evening alone. What was his current mistress like—blonde, brunette, redhead? Petite, voluptuous, tall? She let the litany run like a river of pain through her head. The one who had replaced her four years ago had been her opposite—a fiery, tempestuous Latino beauty, with a taste for flamboyant, revealing clothes. She'd seen a picture of them together in a gossip magazine at the antenatal clinic. Clearly Xander had got bored with the cool, classic type that she had exemplified, had wanted something more exciting…

She tore her mind away. Xander Anaketos's sexual tastes, both past and present, were of no concern to her.

They never would be again.

The river of pain in her head intensified.

CHAPTER SIX

'SEA!' yelled Joey, beside himself with excitement. 'There, there!'

He pointed through the car window to where a bay of dazzling azure blue had just become visible, fringed with vivid emerald-green, all drenched in the hot glare of the Caribbean sun. They had landed at the small, deserted airport of this tiny Caribbean jewel half an hour ago, and were heading to the coast in a chauffeur-driven car.

Contrary to Clare's apprehensions about the long flight, Joey had revelled in every moment, fascinated with the swivelling leather seats, the seat belts, the huge TV screen, the onboard bathroom, the portholes, the cockpit, the galley, and every other aspect of the private jet that had winged them across the Atlantic. To Clare's astonishment Xander had spent the time exclusively devoting himself to keeping Joey entertained, whether by playing childish computer games with him or doing colouring and jigsaws. It was very different from her memories of travelling with Xander as his mistress. He had either spent flights working at his laptop and his papers—or sweeping her back to the sleeping accommodation for some undivided personal attention.

Now he was giving her his undivided personal *in*attention. He was turned away from her, chatting to Joey, pointing out the sights of the island's landscapes.

'See those big trees, and all the round fruits dangling off them like they're on bits of string? Those are mangoes—you'll like mangoes. We'll have some for breakfast. They're very juicy and sweet. And those trees there are banana trees. Do you know something funny about bananas?'

Joey shook his head, eyes wide.

'They grow upside down. I'll show you when we're at the villa.'

Clare was staring bleakly out of her window. She'd been twice to the Caribbean with Xander. Not, thank God, to this island, but even without direct memories just being in the Caribbean was painful. Most of the time she'd been with Xander had been spent travelling with him. He had constantly been doing business. Only occasionally had he pulled the plug on his business affairs and actually had a holiday. Their two visits to the Caribbean had been such. They'd stayed at the kind of five-star boutique hideaway hotel that was written about in the Sunday newspapers with breathless awe at what money could buy, surrounded by exclusively rich and beautiful people—the men rich, the women beautiful.

But Xander had hardly treated those stays as holidays. Oh, he had kept her at his side, both by day and by night, but he had remained in constant communication with his staff and had struck, she knew, at least one business deal with his fellow guests.

How much would Joey see of him now? she wondered. It was one thing to visit Vi's house, another to live for two weeks with a little child in a secluded villa.

The car swept through an iron-gated entrance and along a gravelled drive between lush vegetation, to pull up outside a long, low building. As they got out of the car, the humid warmth enveloped her. Beautifully kept gardens, brilliant with hibiscus and bougainvillaea, surrounded the villa, and already she could see the flashing dart of a hummingbird amongst the vivid blossoms.

She took Joey by the hand and followed Xander inside into a cool air-conditioned interior, with a high, cathedral ceiling, and through huge glass doors to a terrace, beyond which Joey immediately spotted the sea again. He cried out excitedly, and tugged on Clare's hand.

Xander turned and held his hand out.

'Let's hit the beach, Joey,' he said with a grin.

Clare felt pain stab through her. It hurt to see Xander smile like that. A carefree, boyish grin. He was not a man who smiled easily.

'You'll need beach clothes, pet,' she said to Joey. 'And sunblock.'

She led him off to find the bedroom, not caring what Xander wanted. Her luggage, such as it was, was already in the bedroom the smiling maid showed her to, and it did not take long to get herself into shorts and T-shirt and Joey into swimming shorts and a top and hat to protect him from the sun. He protested over the sunblock, but she was adamant.

From the verandah on to which her room opened she could see Xander, standing by an azure swimming pool. He, too, had changed for the beach, and Joey ran down towards him. She followed reluctantly, her cheap flip-flops flapping on the stone paving. She watched as Xander gave Joey another grin, took his hand, and headed down the path to the beach.

Clare might as well not have been there.

Pain stabbed again. To be so cut out—as if she did not exist…

Doggedly, she followed the two receding figures. The moment he could, Joey slipped Xander's hand and ran down over the silvered sand into the crystal-clear turquoise water. As she walked onto the beach, Clare looked around her.

It really was like something out of a brochure for paradise. The long, low villa, set into jewelled gardens, the white sliver of beach, fringed by coconut palms whose fronds were swaying in the gently lifting breeze, and everywhere, stretching to the horizon, the fantastic brilliance of the turquoise sea. Far out, she could see waves splashing on a reef, creating the mirrored pond of the lagoon within.

But she would have given anything not to have been here…

'Mummy! Come in the water!' Joey's voice was high-pitched with excitement.

She waded in with her sandalled feet, feeling the cool water like a balm. Joey jumped up and down, then sat down with a splash.

'You see how happy he is?' Xander's voice was accusatory. 'Yet you would have deprived him of this—as you deprived him of a father.'

Her eyes hardened. 'Don't try and make me feel guilty, Xander!'

Something moved in his face. Then it had gone. In its place was a different expression.

'This isn't good for Joey. All this aggression. He'll pick up on it and it will upset him.'

Clare just looked at him. Her face was stony. How could she possibly endure two weeks here, like this? For a long moment Xander returned her gaze, level and unreadable.

'We're going to have to talk,' he said. 'Tonight, when Joey is in bed.' He turned away, returning his attention to Joey. 'OK, Joey—I'm coming in. Prepare for some serious splashing!'

Xander peeled off his top in a single fluid movement, and without her volition Clare's eyes went to him. Her breath caught, and she was humiliatingly grateful for her dark glasses.

His body was as perfect, as fantastic, as she had remembered it. The smooth, strong-muscled torso, the broad shoulders, the long, lean thighs, hazed lightly with dark hair. As he ran down into the water past her, her eyes went to the perfect sculpture of his back, the narrow form of his hips.

Memory burned, like a wound in her flesh, vivid and excoriating. Once she had held him in her arms. Once that taut, muscled flesh had been hers to caress, hers to yield to, hers to crush herself against.

And now?

He was gone for ever. Beyond her for ever.

She turned away, heading back up towards the terrace.

This holiday would be a season in hell for her.

CHAPTER SEVEN

JOEY was asleep, his bed drawn next to hers, his teddy tucked in beside him. Jet lag had finally overcome him, despite his state of excitement at being here on holiday—and at the wonderful new addition to his life.

As Clare smoothed his dark hair gently, a heaviness of heart pressed on her.

How could two people react so differently to another one? Joey's pleasure and excitement at Xander's presence in his life shone from his eyes. While she dreaded every moment in his company.

And now she was going to have to face him again, without even Joey to dilute the hideous tension she felt.

Another round of Xander's virulent hostility to endure. What would it be this time? she thought bitterly. More trying to make her feel bad for not having told him she was pregnant? More lectures on Joey's right to a father? Or, worst of all, more insane proposals like their getting married?

At least he'd backed off on that one. Maybe even he now saw the insanity of it. Cold ran down her spine at the memory of him coolly informing her he was going to marry her—

Marriage to him would be as agonising now as it would have been four years ago. Nothing could change that...

She straightened and left the room, checking the baby monitor was on and taking the handset with her. As she walked back along the terrace she could hear the cicadas in the bushes, the occasional piercing chirrup of a tree frog, and feel the encircling warmth of the tropical night embrace her. She was still warm, even in shorts and T-shirt. She hadn't bothered to change. What for?

Who for?

Not for Xander, that was for sure.

Never again for him.

The heaviness in her heart crushed her yet more.

The swift Caribbean night had fallen. The sky to the west carried the faint remains of blueness, while in the east brilliant gold stars were pricking through the floor of heaven.

The beauty of the setting mocked her.

So, too, even more cruelly, did the beauty of the man waiting for her, in an old-fashioned steamer chair set on the lawn near the pool, his legs stretched out, a bottle of cold beer in his grip. He looked at her as she walked towards him.

She felt suddenly acutely self-conscious. There was something in the way he was watching her that had nothing to do with the way he had regarded her since their fateful, nightmare encounter in the cocktail lounge.

Heavily, she plonked herself down in the other steamer. Almost instantly one of the house staff was there, enquiring politely what she would like to drink. She asked for a fruit punch, and it was there moments later, served in a beautiful expensive glass, with slices of fresh fruit and a frosted rim. She took a sip and frowned. It had alcohol in it—rum, probably. For an instant she thought to return it, then shrugged mentally. She could probably do with some Dutch courage.

She looked across at Xander.

'Well?' she said. She might as well get this over with. 'You wanted to talk, so talk.'

For a second he said nothing. Then he spoke. 'You've changed. I would hardly have known you.'

Even in the dusk she could feel a flush in her cheeks as his glance levelled at her assessingly.

'Well, that's hardly surprising,' she retorted. 'My lifestyle's a little different,' she said sarcastically.

He gave a quick shake of his head. 'I don't mean your looks.

That's understandable. I mean you.' He paused, looking at her. 'You're—harder.'

She gave a snort. 'Depends on the company,' she said. She took a mouthful of the rum punch. The alcohol kicked through her.

His eyes narrowed. 'So this is the real you I'm seeing now? I never saw it before.'

No, she thought, because I wasn't like that then. I was— stupid. Trusting. Hopeful.

Stupid.

Well, so what? That was then, this was now. She took another drink from her cocktail, and stared across at Xander.

'I thought you wanted to talk about Joey,' she demanded

He didn't like her speaking to him like that, she could see. But she didn't care. He was right—she wasn't the same person she had been when she'd been his mistress. She *was* harder now. She'd had to be. Had to be ever since the moment she'd murmured, 'Will you excuse me a moment?' to him in the restaurant at the St John and walked out of his life. Taking the marching orders he'd just handed her with brutal suddenness.

'Obviously,' he answered brusquely. 'What else would we have to talk about?' For a second, the very briefest second, there was a shift in his eyes. Then it was gone. 'Like I told you—this aggression is not good for him. It's got to stop.'

She stared at him. 'So stop it,' she said.

His mouth tightened. He definitely did not like being spoken to like that. Then, visibly, he made his expression impassive.

'For Joey's sake, I will. And so will you.'

For a moment Clare wanted to bite back that she did not take orders. Then she subsided. Joey would only be upset if he realised how much hostility there was between the two people who had created him.

'OK,' she conceded. 'In front of Joey.'

He shook his head.

'Not good enough. It's not something you can turn on and off, whenever he's around or not. It's got to be permanent.'

She just looked at him. Looked at the man who had deleted her from his bed—his life—in a single sentence. With brutal words. A man she had actually thought felt for her something that went beyond her role as his mistress.

But all he had felt for her had been 'appreciation'.

Appreciation that he had paid for with a diamond necklace.

'How the hell,' she said heavily, 'do you think that's possible?'

Again there was that brief flicker in his eyes. Then it was gone.

'By forcing ourselves,' he replied. 'Until it becomes a habit. Because this isn't going to go away. *I* am not going to go away. I'm going to be part of my son's life for ever—and you'd better accept that. This is what I propose—'

She snorted again. 'Not another insane idea like the last one, I hope?'

Again came that strange, very fleeting expression in his eyes, which she could hardly see in this dim light.

'No. For Joey's sake we behave…normally…with each other. Putting everything else aside. And we can start right now.' He got to his feet. 'Over dinner.'

He indicated the terrace, and Clare could see that the table there had been set for a meal, with flowers and napery and soft candles. Xander was looking at her. She headed towards it, rum punch in her hand, and plonked herself down, flicking her plait over her shoulder.

He took his place opposite her. It seemed a whole lot too close for Clare's liking.

'Your hair is longer,' he said.

'Long hair's cheaper than short,' she answered.

'Why do you wear it constrained like that in a…a pigtail all the time?'

She looked at him. 'It keeps it out of the way when I'm busy.'

'Well, you are on holiday now. You don't have to be busy. You can relax. Let your hair down.'

His eyes flicked over her. In the pit of her stomach Clare felt desire begin to pool.

The appearance of the steward was a reprieve, and the whole formal rigmarole of serving dinner gave her the insulation she needed. Wine and water was poured, bread was proffered, plates deposited with gloved hands. This might be a villa by the sea, but it was a silver service. No doubt.

Sickly she realised that the last time she had sat having dinner with Xander it had been the night she had been terminated.

He had seemed preoccupied then—and with hindsight, of course, it had been obvious why. He hadn't even wanted to be there—had simply been waiting for the moment to hit the delete button on her...

She glanced across at him now. Four years ago. Had it really been so long? It seemed much, much closer in time than that.

But it wasn't—it was four years ago. Four years—and everything changed that night. Your whole life. And nothing—not even Xander Anaketos storming back to claim his fatherhood of Joey—will change it back. Nothing.

She started to eat.

It was a strained, bizarre meal. Xander made conversation. Deliberately so, she realized. Perhaps partly for the waiting staff, but also because he was following his own precepts and trying to give an appearance of normality to their dining. He talked of the island—a little of its history as a former colony, and the activities it afforded those rich enough to holiday here. Clare returned the barest replies, a feeling of unreality seeping through her.

She tried not to look at him, tried not to hear that naturally seductive timbre in his voice, tried not to catch the scent of his skin. She had to stop herself, she knew. But it was a torment.

I've got to get used to this. I have no other option. So if I'm to endure it, I must make myself immune to it. To him.

It was with a sense of relief that she felt herself yawn at the end of the main course. She pushed her chair back. The glass of wine she'd sipped almost without realising it, combined with jet lag, was knocking her out fast.

'I'm falling asleep,' she said. 'I'm going to go to bed.'

Did that slightest flicker come again? She didn't know, didn't care—was too tired to think about it.

'I'll see you in the morning,' he murmured, and reached for his own wine glass.

She left him to it and headed indoors. The cool of the air-conditioning made her shiver after the warmth outdoors.

Or something did.

Behind her, Xander watched her go. His expression was strange. His mood stranger. She had changed, all right—she was a different woman from the one he remembered. The one who had been so reserved she had refused to look at him as he walked past the time he'd first spotted her at his London offices. The one who had become his mistress without a murmur, her cool, understated beauty engaging his interest as an intriguing contrast to the sophisticated passions of the previous incumbent, whose charms had palled for him. Clare had fitted into his life effortlessly, and he had taken her with him because she'd been undemanding and accommodating, calm and composed—the classic English rose without thorns...

His mouth twisted. Well, that had gone, and with a vengeance! Now she scratched and tore at him verbally, snapped and snarled and answered back, defying him and refusing to do what was best for his son. His expression darkened. Would she realise why he had brought her here? He lifted the wine to his mouth and savoured its rich, expensive bouquet. His eyes glinted opaquely.

Not until it's far, far too late for her...

CHAPTER EIGHT

CLARE sat on a padded lounger on the beach, under the shade of a coconut palm, looking out over the brilliant azure water beyond the silver sand.

She had been here a week. The most difficult week of her life. Even the days after Xander had thrown her out of his life, even when she had given birth to his child, even the nightmare of coming face to face with him again, did not compare with this.

Each passing day here seemed more difficult than the last. She tried her hardest not to let it show for Joey's sake—to be calm and normal, to conceal from him the emotions roiling in the pit of her stomach, to speak civilly to Xander so that Joey would not be upset. But it was hard, so hard.

But only for her, it seemed. Joey, she could see with her own eyes, day after day, was having the time of his life—and so was Xander.

Her eyes went to the two figures in the sea, one so small, battling with his armbands, the other tall and bronzed and lithe. She watched Joey throwing a huge inflated ball at Xander, who made a vastly exaggerated play of launching himself sideways to catch it, landing in the water with an almighty splash. Joey whooped with laughter and Xander surfaced, his grin wide, shaking water drops from his head.

Clare felt her hands tighten around her book. Watching them together sent a pain through her heart she could not stop.

Could that really be Xander Anaketos there? Playing with his little child? It was a man she had never seen before. Xander as she had never known him. A man who—pain pierced her—had existed only in her imagination, for so brief and pathetic a time, when she had hoped against hope that he felt something for her, that when she told him the news that she was pregnant he would sweep her up into his arms and declare his love for her—marry her, make them a family together...

That dream had been obliterated for ever in a single moment.

'It's over.'

Pain stabbed again, the deepest yet. All she had was this hollow mockery—three people who looked like a family but who were no such thing...

'Mummy! Mummy! Come in the water!'

Joey's excited voice called to her. He was wading out, running across the sand to her. He seized her hand. 'Come on, Mummy,' he said, and started to drag at her.

'Your mother wants to rest, Joey.' Xander's deep voice sounded as he came up to Joey, ready to lead him back to the sea. Water ran from his sleek, bare torso, dazzling like diamonds. Clare did not want to look.

Joey's expression grew doleful. 'It's no fun resting,' he objected. 'Come on, Mummy.'

Clare got to her feet. 'Of course I'll come in,' she said. There was no point lying there, heart heavy.

Joey seized her hand enthusiastically, then grabbed Xander's hand.

'Swing me!' he commanded.

Automatically Clare raised her arm, as did Xander.

'One, two, three, *swing!*' ordered Joey.

She hefted him up, and Xander did too.

'Whee!' cried Joey. 'Again, again!'

'One, two, three, *swing!*' said Clare, hefting Joey up again, and realised that she had said it in unison with Xander. Her eyes flew to his, and just for a moment, the briefest moment, they met. Then she tore her eyes away.

Emotion buckled through her.

Suddenly, out of nowhere, it seemed unbearable—just unbearable. To be here, Joey's mother and father, so close to him, with him linking them together, and yet to be so unbridgeably far apart.

'Swing me into the water!'

'You'll have to run, then,' said Xander. He glanced at Clare. 'Ready?' he said.

She nodded. They ran, all three of them, down into the water, and at the last moment they lifted him up and up, then swung him out and let him go in the deeper water. He gave a squeal of glee as he splashed down.

Clare laughed. She could not stop herself. She felt Xander's eyes on her as well, and suddenly he gave a laugh too, plunging forward to scoop up Joey.

'Throw me again, Daddy!'

Xander laughed, and tossed him once more into the water with a huge splash.

And now Clare wasn't laughing. She felt, of all things, her throat constrict and tears start in her eyes.

He was good with Joey—so *good*! The evidence could not be denied. Full of fun, laughter and, most piercingly painful of all, affection. And she knew, with a deep hollowing of her stomach, full of love. Love for Joey. His son.

And Joey loved him, too. She could see that—could not deny it. And how should it not be? He was a father any child would adore.

Memory came to her out of the years so long ago. A beach holiday with her parents. She'd only been little, how old she could not remember, but she remembered her parents, running down into the sea with her, how happy she had been…

I should have told him—I should have told him I was pregnant. I should have taken the risk and lived with it. He had a right to know, and Joey had a right to a father.

The self-accusation burned in her. Xander might not be capable of love for her—perhaps not for any woman—but he was capable of love for Joey. And she must accept it. Whatever it cost her, however cruel the fate she had been left with. The fate of knowing that all she could have was this bitter mockery—to see Xander with Joey, so warm and loving, and know that she was forever excluded.

And another torment too. One that was twisting in her day after day, night after night. For if the days were bad—when she had to watch Xander and Joey forge their new bond together, a bond that shut her out—the evenings were even worse. Because every evening, when Joey was asleep, she had to endure the ritual torture of dining with Xander.

And that was the worst of all. For the most awful of reasons.

Anguish flashed in her eyes.

Why? *Why* was it so hard? It should be getting easier, not harder! Day after day of seeing Xander again—surely it should be getting easier to endure? She should be getting more immune to him, day by day—surely she should?

And yet she wasn't. Her helpless, crippling awareness of him was increasing. It was a torment—a terror. Everything about him drew her eye—made her punishingly aware of him.

During the day she could fight it—she had Joey's presence to strengthen her. But over dinner... Oh, then, dear God, it was an excruciating torment. For him to be so close to her, a few feet away across the table—and yet further from her than if he had been on the moon.

She had tried to fight it, but it was so hard, so impossible. While she had been able to resort to open hostility it had been a bulwark, a barrier against him. But now—

I don't want to want him!

As she stared out over the beach, let her eyes run with helpless longing over his lean, muscled torso, feast on the sculpted features of his face, caught her breath as he threw back his sable head and laughed, she felt her stomach clench unbearably and knew the truth that terrified her.

She still wanted Xander Anaketos.

Whatever he had done to her—she still wanted him.

Xander lifted his wine glass and looked across the table at Clare. Turbid emotion, laced with memory, swirled within him, but he ignored it. The past was gone, over. It was the present he had to deal with. And the absolute priority right now was to achieve his goal. He would do so. He had no doubt. He had always achieved his goals in life. He would now, too—whatever it took. Too much was at stake. His son's future.

His son…

As he had done time after time, whenever those words rang in his head, he felt his heart turn over. Catch and swell with pride and love. How was it possible that he should feel so strongly? Emotion had never figured much in his life. He had had no use for it, no need of it, and he had always kept it at bay, taking whatever steps necessary to do so. Irony flickered briefly, then he brushed it aside, as an irrelevance that he could do without. And yet when he had set eyes on Joey, recognised him as his son, his reaction had been overwhelming. In an instant his son had become the overriding imperative of his life.

Every day he spent with Joey only made him more determined that he would spend his life with him. And how he achieved that did not matter. Only his son's happiness mattered. And Joey *was* happy—every grin, every excited cry of glee, told him that. There was no sign, none at all, that Joey sensed any hostility between his parents.

He watched as Clare crumbled a piece of bread in her fingers. He had demanded a cessation of hostilities and she had complied. He granted her that. From the outside they must look like a normal family on holiday.

His mouth twisted. How deceptive appearances could be.

And yet…

Xander's fingers tightened momentarily around the stem of his wine glass. That moment today, when they had swung Joey into the water, for a few fleeting moments they had acted in unison, as if it were normal, natural to do so. As if the appearance was, even for a brief moment, the reality.

His eyes rested on his son's mother.

Four years since she had been in his life.

She had changed, indeed. Or had she merely revealed the person she had always been, having concealed it from him when she was his mistress? He had called her harder now than when he had first known her, and with him that was true—and yet with Joey she was as soft as butter. Emotions warred within him. What she had done was unforgivable—to keep his son from him, to deny Joey his father. And yet all the evidence of his eyes, both in London and now here, day after day, was that she was devoted as a mother. Warm and loving. Affectionate and demonstrative.

A good mother.

He had to allow her that, begrudge it though he did. And for his son's sake, he had to be grateful. Even though the disparity between how she was with Joey and everything else he knew about her was so discordant.

He frowned inwardly. With Joey he saw her being someone he had never seen before. A different woman from the one he'd known four years ago. As his mistress she had always been so cool, so detached, so undemonstrative. As his mistress he had found it highly erotic—knowing that, for all her outward composure, all he had to do was touch her and she would come alive at his touch. Within seconds she would be quivering with passion. It had been a powerful fascination for him, the contrast between her public self and the private one that he could arouse in her.

That alone had been enough to justify why he had kept her so much longer than any other mistress.

For a moment his eyes shadowed, as he remembered again the moment when he had finished with her. When she had got to her feet and walked calmly out of his life. Carrying his child away with her out of spite for being discarded.

No. He set his glass down with a click on the surface of the table. There was no point going there. No purpose in revisiting the past. It was the present he had to deal with—and the future. That was all that was important. Right now, only his son's happiness was important—and he would take whatever measures necessary to safeguard that happiness.

Whatever measures necessary…

His eyes rested on the woman who had once been his mistress, and he focussed his mind on the task ahead. She had been responsive to him then—oh, so responsive!—and neither the passage of four years, nor the splenetic anger she had unleashed on him, nor her cursed vindictiveness towards him by keeping his son from him, had changed that. He'd had proof, every day they'd been here, with no room for her to shut him out, ignore him, escape him.

Exactly the proof he wanted.

He eased his shoulders and lounged back in his chair as the staff served dinner. Opposite him, Clare sat stiffly. But her eyes had followed his movement, he knew. Surreptitiously, but discernibly. He could see her eyes following him and then flicking away, the way she didn't want to meet his eyes, the way she pulled herself away from him if he got too close. Her whole body language and behaviour with him betrayed her.

Well, that was good—very good. Just what he wanted.

Excitement flared briefly in him, but he suppressed it. In its place he forced himself to look at her with impassive objectivity.

Four years on her beauty had matured. Even without her making the slightest attempt to improve on nature by way of make-up, hairstyling or clothes, her beauty revealed itself. Beneath the cheap fabric of her T-shirt he could see the soft swell of her breasts, and her chainstore shorts could not disguise the slenderness of her waist and hips, the long smooth curve of her thighs.

He felt the shimmer of sexual arousal ease through him.

A sliver of emotion broke through the barrier he'd imposed.

Can I really go through with this?

For a moment doubt possessed him. Then he freed himself.

He would do what he intended.

For his son's sake.

Tonight was the worst yet. Clare sat, tension racking through every limb, and picked at the exquisitely presented food in front of her. It felt so wrong not to appreciate it more, but she had no appetite. Maybe too much sun?

But she knew that wasn't the reason she had no appetite— wasn't the reason she kept taking repeated unwise sips from her wine, even after she'd fortified herself with the rum punch that she was diligently handed every evening as she emerged from seeing Joey to sleep.

The reason she felt so strangely weak, so hazed, was not

because of the sun. It was because of the man sitting opposite her. The man who was lifting his wine glass to his lips with a lounging grace that sent a tremor through her veins. The man whose long legs were stretched out underneath the table, so close to hers that she had to inch them away, awkwardly shifting her position.

The man whose gaze was resting on her now, with an expression she could not read.

She took a forkful of food and tried to chew it, but it was hard to swallow. She washed it down with another mouthful of wine and set the fork back on the plate, letting it be.

'You don't like the fish?'

Xander's enquiry, civilly made, but with the slightest lazy drawl in it, drew a quick shake of the head from her.

'I'm just not hungry,' she said.

'The chef will cook you something else. You only have to say.'

'No—no, thank you.'

She took another sip of wine—for something to do. She could feel the effects of the alcohol and knew she should not drink any more. Yet it seemed to give her the strength she knew she needed. She took another sip, turning her head to gaze out over the softly lit pool and the glimmering sea beyond. She could just make out the shape of the palm fronds, outlined against the sky.

It was so beautiful.

Idyllic.

Idyllic to be here, on this beautiful tropical island, with the warmth kissing her body, the softest breeze playing with her hair, the coil of wine in her blood easing through her veins.

She gazed out over the view, dim in the starlight and the shimmer of the pool lights.

Her thoughts were strange.

Unreal.

Slowly she drank more wine.

Across the table she could hear the chink of Xander's knife and fork, but he did not talk to her.

She was glad. Their stilted, deliberate conversations over dinner this last week had been an ordeal for her. Silence was easier.

She eased back in the chair, stretching out her legs, and kept on gazing out to sea. She could hear the waves, murmuring on the shore, the wind soughing softly in the palms, the soporific song of the cicadas.

Her body felt warm from the heat of the day. Warm and languorous.

She felt herself easing more in her chair, stretching out her legs yet more.

Lifting the wine glass to her lips.

It was empty.

Curious, she thought, and twisted her slender fingers around its stem, slowly replacing it on the table.

Xander was watching her.

He'd stopped eating. He was sitting there in his chair, very still. His eyes were narrowed, very slightly narrowed.

Memory hollowed within her like a caverning space, enveloping time. She knew that look—knew it in the core of her body, in the sudden pulse of her blood. Her eyes locked to his. Locked, and were held.

She could not move. Could only feel the heat of her body start to spread, like a long, low flush. Could only feel her heart in her chest start to beat with long, low slugs, a drum beating out a slow, insistent message that she knew—oh, she knew.

Xander got to his feet. She watched him, eyes still locked to his, as he came around the end of the table to where she sat. He reached down his hand to her.

And, ever so slowly, she put her hand in his.

He drew her to her feet.

For one last, long moment his eyes stayed locked to hers. And then the dark sweep of his lashes dipped and his head lowered.

His lips were velvet on hers, touching her with liquid smoothness, dissolving through her. It was bliss—honeyed, sweetest bliss—and she felt her eyes flutter shut as she gave herself to the exquisite sensation. With infinite skill he played with her mouth, and yet with every touch his kiss deepened, strengthened. Somehow—she did not know how, could not tell—his hands had folded around her, one splayed across her spine at her waist, one at the tender nape of her neck, holding her for him.

She felt herself sinking, yielding to the sensations he was arousing in her.

From touch…exquisite touch.

And, more potent still, from memory.

Because her body remembered. Remembered as if four years had never been. Instinctively, as if she had always, always been in his arms, his embrace. As if no time had passed at all. As if it had dissolved at his liquid touch.

How long she stood there, with his hands gliding down the length of her spine while his mouth gave play to hers, softly, arousingly, oh, so arousingly, she did not know. Did not know when it was that she felt the strong columns of his thighs pressing against hers, guiding her, turning her, or when his hand slid to hers, folding it within his fingers as his mouth, still dipping low over hers, drew back enough for him to start to lead her—lead her to where she could only ache to go.

She was helpless, she knew. Knew somewhere in the last frail remnants of her mind that she could not stop, could not halt what was happening to her. Could only go where she was being led, along the terrace to another door, another room, a room with a wide, luxurious bed. He was guiding her towards it, his mouth dipping to hers, tasting her, caressing her, arousing her…

And she was responding. She felt the heat flow in her veins, flushing through her skin, warming her with its soft, insistent fire. She could feel herself quickening, tightening, tautening—her body's responses feeding off him, off itself. Her breathing quickened too, her pulse beginning to beat more rapidly.

He was lowering her down upon soft sheets already drawn back by the maids, the pillow yielding as her head pressed down, his mouth still on hers.

Her hands were on his back, and as the hard muscles and flesh indented to her fingers she felt memory flood back into her head like a racing tide.

Oh, dear God, it was Xander—Xander in her arms again, Xander's mouth on hers, his hands caressing her, his strong, lean body pressing down on hers. Desire was unleashed within her, and hunger, such a hunger, ravening and desperate, to have him, to hold him, to touch him and possess him—to give herself to him.

Swiftly, he pulled off her T-shirt, and she lifted her arms to let him, and in the same skilled movement his fingers had slipped the fastening of her bra. It was falling loose, loosening its burden within, so that her breasts spilled into his returning hands.

Her back arched in pleasure as her breasts filled his grasp, and then, as his thumb teased over the instantly stiffening peaks, a low, long moan came from her throat.

How could she have forgotten such bliss? How could she have lived without it? It was ecstasy, it was heaven, it was everything she had ever wanted, could ever want. The low, gasping moan came again, and as if it had been a signal his hands went from her breasts to her waist, lifting her hips, sliding down the unnecessary covering of her clothes. And then his body was against hers. He was naked. How had that happened? She did not know, did not care—knew only that her hips were lifting to him even while at her breasts his mouth was lowering.

Sensation flooded through her. The exquisite arousal of his tongue, slowly circling the straining peaks of her nipples, shot with a million darts of pleasure, making her neck arch back, her lips part.

She wanted more, and yet more. An infinity of more! Her body knew and was asking for it, craving it, hungering for it, hips lifting to him, wanting him—oh, wanting him so much, so much…

She could feel herself flooding, dewing with desire, and she could feel him, feel the seeking tip of his velvet shaft. Excitement burst through her, more intense, more urgent than ever, and she gave again that low moan of longing in her throat.

His head lifted from her breast. For one long, endless moment his eyes looked into hers. In the dimness she could not see his face, only the faint outline of his features, only the glint of light in the eyes that held hers—held hers as slowly, with infinite control, while she gazed wildly, helplessly up at him, her body flushed and aching for him, he came down on her.

He filled her completely, in one slow, engorging stroke, and as she parted for him, took him in, it was if she had melded to him, become one with him.

Her hands convulsed around his back, her hips straining against his.

He was saying something, whispering Greek words she did not understand. She knew only that suddenly, out of nowhere, the rhythm had changed, that suddenly, out of nowhere, he was moving again within her—not slowly now, but urgently, desperately.

She answered him—meeting each thrusting stroke with her own body, clutching at him with her hands, her shoulders lifting from the pillows, bowing herself towards him, legs locking around him.

She cried out, and what she cried she did not know—knew only that she wanted him, *needed* him to hold her. He held her so closely as he thrust into her, deeper and more deeply yet, until he struck the very centre of her being. The very heart of her.

And she cried out again.

A cry stifled as his mouth caught hers, as her body caught fire from his. It sheeted through her body, white-hot, searing with a sensation so intense it was as if never until this moment had she existed.

It went on and on, flooding through time, dissolving it as if it did not exist. Burning away everything that had come between them. Emotion swept through her, overwhelming and overpowering. Filling her, flooding her.

She knew, without uncertainty or doubt, without hesitation or resistance, what that emotion was.

And as the realisation gaped through her she realised the most terrible truth in the world.

She was still in love with Xander Anaketos.

CHAPTER NINE

CLARE lay in his arms. She could do nothing else. She had no strength to move. No strength of body or of soul. She lay quite still, her head resting on his chest, his arm around her shoulder, his hand lying slackly on her upper arm, his legs still half tangled with hers.

She disengaged, her body slipping from his, indenting heavily into the mattress, as her heart-rate began to slow, her heated flesh to cool.

What had she done? What madness, insanity had possessed her?

And—more than that—what criminal stupidity had she committed?

They lay there, two people—two completely dissociated people. Lying there, flesh against flesh, hers soft and exhausted, his hard and muscled, bathed in a faint, cooling sheen of sweat, chilling in the air-conditioned atmosphere.

But she didn't care about the cold.

It echoed the chill inside her head, where her mind was very slowly repeating, like an endless replay, the same question.

What have I done? What have I done?

She went on lying there, her mind barely working, as if shut down or on standby. Because there was a program running that was taking up all her brain—only she could not let it out into her consciousness. Yet it was growing all the time, consuming more resources, more space, consuming everything she was.

She stared out blindly into the dark room.

Was he asleep? There was no movement—none—from the

body beside her, only the subdued rise and fall of his chest. She waited, hearing through her bones the uneven slug of her own heart—unquiet, unresting.

Quietly she slid from the bed. He still did not move. Carefully, shakily, she picked up her discarded clothes, not finding her bra, not caring—caring only that she pulled on her shorts, pulled on her T-shirt, covered her nakedness.

And she went. Fleeing from the scene of her crime, her unspeakable folly.

She slipped out onto the terrace, the humid warmth of the tropical night hitting her like a wall. For a moment she gasped in the steamy air, as if unable to breathe, and then, swallowing hard, made her way to her own room. Inside, she ran for the bathroom.

The shower was hot—as hot as she could stand it. Washing her. Washing everything from her.

Everything but the knowledge of what she had done.

Then, like a wounded animal, she crawled to her bed.

Beside her, undisturbed, her son lay sleeping. The fruit of her folly. The folly of being in love with Xander Anaketos—for which folly she must now pay the same killing price she had paid before.

Out over the water nothing stirred—except the faint, far-off sound of the sea on the reef. Behind Xander the incessant cicadas kept up their sussurating chorus, and in the palms above his head the night wind soughed. Somewhere a lone dog barked, and fell silent.

Xander stood staring sightlessly out to sea, to the dark horizon beyond. He had waited until she had gone, lying in the simulation of sleep. Then he had got out of bed, unable to stay there longer. Pulled on his jeans and walked out here, into the darkness. The warmth of the tropical night lapped him, yet he felt cold. He plunged his hands further into the pockets of his jeans, roughly drawn on, his torso still bare, like his feet.

The coldness was all the way through him. Chilling him to the core.

He had done what he had set out to do. Achieved his goal.

He should be pleased. Satisfied.

Relieved.

He felt none of these things.

Only that he had made a terrible, catastrophic mistake.

'I've eaten my breakfast. Come and play, Daddy!'

Joey beamed invitingly. He seemed completely—thank-fully—oblivious to the atmosphere at the table.

You could cut it like a knife, thought Clare, her face expressionless. She was moving like a mummy, wrapped up so tightly that she was almost incapable of moving. There were circles under her eyes from a sleepless, self-lacerating night.

Joey had woken at his customary early hour, and she had gone with him, like an automaton, to make their customary early-morning inspection of the gardens and walk along the beach till breakfast. Usually it was the time she almost enjoyed—so quiet, in the coolest time of the day, and safe from Xander, whom she would not see till breakfast. It was a time when she had Joey all to herself and could almost forget just how totally her life had changed now. How disastrously.

But this morning the walk along the beach had been torture. Hell in the middle of paradise.

The beauty of the island had mocked her mercilessly, showing her cruelly, pitilessly, with every glint of sunlight off the azure water, every curve of the emerald-fringed bay, every grain of soft, silvery sand, just how misery could dwell in the midst of beauty.

Now, as she sat at the breakfast table, she could not let her eyes go near Xander. Could say nothing to him. Could not bear to be near him. Yet she had to. For Joey's sake she had to make everything appear normal, though the mockery of it screamed at her in her head. Her awareness of his presence was like a radio tuned to a pitch that was like fingernails scraping. Every move he made, every terse syllable he spoke in response to Joey's artless chatter, every breath that came from him, vibrated in the air between them.

She was completely incapable of eating anything. She had forced down some sips of coffee through a tight, constricted throat, and that was all. Now, as Joey beamed so invitingly at Xander, she thought, desperately, Please, yes. Take him off and play with him. Go, just go—anywhere, but away from me, away from me…

'Not right now, Joey. Soon.'

Clare scraped her chair back. If Xander would not clear off, then she would. Must.

'I'll play, Joey,' she said, her voice stiff and expressionless. She held her hand out to help Joey down. But he looked at her mutinously.

'I want Daddy,' he said. His lower lip wobbled. Maybe he was not so immune to the tension stretching like hot wires between her and Xander after all, Clare realised heavily. She saw Xander press the service button on the table. A moment later the house-keeper appeared.

'Juliette, would be you be kind enough to amuse Joey for a while, please?' he said to her. His voice sounded as tense as Clare's.

Juliette gave a warm smile, and then bestowed an even warmer one on Joey.

'You come with Juliette, now. I happen to know…' she looked conspiratorial '…that it's car wash day this morning—and there's a hose with your name on it!'

Joey's lower lip stopped wobbling instantly. He scrambled down eagerly.

'I need a *big* hose,' he informed Juliette as she led him off.

Clare watched him go. He was out of sight before she turned her head back. What was going on? Why had Xander got rid of Joey?

Oh, God, he doesn't think we're going to have sex again, does he?

The thought plunged, horrifically, into her brain, and her eyes lashed to Xander's face before she could stop herself. But whatever was on his mind, that was not it. She looked away again instantly and felt relief flood through her, drowning out any other reaction she might have had to that sudden debilitating thought.

Over and over again during the long, agonising night she had asked herself the same question—why, *why* had he done it? Why had he wanted sex with her last night?

And there was only one answer.

Because right now she was the only woman around. And she was better than nothing. There was no other reason he could possibly have had. None.

Loathing shot through her. For him, for doing that to her, and—worse by far—loathing for herself. For having been so crushingly, unforgivably stupid as to let him…

'Clare—'

Her name jolted her, and her eyes went to him involuntarily.

His face was expressionless. Quite expressionless. And yet there was something so far at the back of his eyes that she had seen once before…

And suddenly, deep inside her, fear opened up. She knew that face. Knew this moment. Recognised it from four long years ago, when she had sat in the restaurant at the St John and heard her life destroyed—her hopes decimated—in one brutal sentence.

But this time she was no longer the person she had been then. Harder. Xander had called her that to her face, and it was true. She'd had to make herself hard, or she would not have survived. Would have bled to death.

How can I love him?

The cry came from deep inside, anguished and unanswerable.

How can I love a man who threw me out like rubbish, who packed me off with a diamond necklace, who last night used me for sex because I was convenient and on hand…?

How can I love a man like that? A man without feelings, without conscience, without remorse, or the slightest acknowledgement that he was so coldly callous to me?

I mustn't love a man like that! It debases me to do so. I thought I was free of him—I made myself free of him. I forced myself to be free of him.

But it had been in vain. Completely in vain. It had all come to nothing that night she had stood face to face again with the man she had loved, but who had never, ever felt anything more for her than 'appreciation' for her sexual services…

The whole excruciating agony of her situation honed in on her like a scud missile. Because of Joey she could never be free of Xander. Never! The nightmare she had feared four years ago had come true—she would be forced to see him, forced to be civil to him and pretend, time after time, year after year, that he could not hurt her any more. For Joey's sake she had to let that happen, had to endure it.

'Clare—what happened last night—'

He stopped, mouth tightening. She stared at him expressionlessly. As blankly as he. But his next words came out of the blue.

'When is your period due?'

'*What?*' Her eyes stared in shock at the question.

His mouth tightened again. 'When is your period due?' he repeated.

She stared at him uncomprehendingly.

'It may have escaped your notice,' he said tightly, 'but last night we had unprotected sex. What are your chances of getting pregnant?'

Faintness drummed through her. She could feel it fuzzing her brain. She pressed her fingers down on the table, willing herself to be calm.

Dear God, do not do this to me—

The silent, despairing plea came from her depths of fear.

'When will you know? Know if you are pregnant?'

'I—' She forced herself to think—think what date it was. With all the turmoil in her life, keeping track of her menstrual cycle was the last thing on her mind.

'At the end of the week, I think,' she said uncertainly.

He got up from the table abruptly.

'Let me know,' he said tersely, and walked away.

For one long, timeless moment Clare sat there. Then, with a strange, choking sound in her throat, she blindly pushed herself up.

She started to walk. Her legs were jerking, but she forced herself. Forced herself to go on. The lawn crunched under her bare feet, the stone of the paving around the pool was hot to her soles, and then there was sand, soft, sinking sand, and she couldn't walk any more. Her feet stumbled on stiff, jerky legs.

She sank to the sand.

Her shoulders began to shake.

Xander heard the scrape of a chair on the terrace and stiffened. Was she coming after him? He half turned his head, tensing.

He didn't want her coming near him. Didn't want her speaking to him. Didn't want her in the same universe as him.

But that wasn't possible. Because of Joey, because of his son, he couldn't get rid of her. And there was nothing, *nothing* he could do about it.

She was a life sentence for him.

He could feel the prison doors closing on him. There was no escape—none.

Emotion churned in him, harsh and pitiless.

She was heading away from him, he saw with grim vision. Walking over the lawn, past the pool, towards the beach. His eyes went to her, and his mouth tightened even more.

Christos—no escape. None!

A life sentence.

He went on watching her walk away from him, with that strange, uneven gait.

Then he saw her falter, sway very slightly, then, with a sudden jerking movement, she folded onto the sand.

He started to move.

Her shoulders were shaking. Through her body huge, agonising shudders were convulsing her. Her throat was so tight she felt it must tear and burst. She wrapped her arms around herself, pulling tighter and tighter. She would fall apart if she did not. The wracking convulsions were shattering her, shaking her to pieces, to tiny fragments.

She took a terrible, agonising draft of breath.

And then the tears came.

She couldn't stop them. They poured out of her, gushing from her eyes with hot, burning salt, choking in her throat, her lungs. She drew up her legs, wrapping her arms tightly around her knees, trying to hold herself together.

But she couldn't. The sobs shook her, raw and rasping, impossible to halt. It was the first time in four years she had cried—and now she couldn't stop.

Her hands pressed around her knees, nails digging into the bare flesh of her thighs. Head buried in her arms, her shoulders convulsed.

She could not bear it. She had reached the end now. There was no more strength in her. Nothing left in her at all.

A shadow fell over her.

'Clare?'

The voice was strange. The strangest voice she'd ever heard. But she could not hear it clearly. The sobs in her throat drowned out everything; the hot, agonising tears blinded her. Her nails digging into her legs was all she could feel, except for the convulsions of her body

'Clare?'

It was that voice again. Stranger still. She did not recognise it. It belonged to someone she did not know. Who did not exist.

The sobs went on, consuming her.

'Clare!'

That voice again, different still, and more words, words she did not understand, sounding urgent. Imperative.

He was beside her, crouching down. His hands were on her shoulders, hunched so tightly, with her arms wrapping around her, holding herself together. His hands went to her head, bent and broken over her knees, forcing it up.

A word broke from him. She did not know what it meant. Could only stare, blindly, through the tears coursing down her cheeks, as the sobs jerked in her throat, her face crumpling, breath gasping.

There was something in his face, his eyes.

It was shock. Raw, naked shock.

'Oh, my God, Clare—why? Why?'

It was the incomprehension in his voice. That was what did it. Her hands flew up. Lashed out, flailing. Hitting and hitting at him on the solid wall of his chest.

'You bastard!'

The invective choked from her, crippling her.

Hands closed about her wrists instantly, in a reflex action. She struggled against his grip, hopeless and helpless, and the sobs were still storming through her.

'What do you mean, "Why?"' she choked. 'How can you say that? After everything you've done to me, you ask Why—like it's some kind of *mystery*?'

His grip on her wrists tightened, and his crouching stance steadied.

'What I've done to you?' he echoed. Suddenly, frighteningly, the expression in his eyes changed, flashing with dark, killing anger. 'You kept my son from me! Nothing, *nothing* justifies that. You've had *four years* to tell me I have a son. But you never did and you were never going to. I was going to live not knowing about Joey—*never* knowing about him!'

Her face contorted, but not from weeping this time.

'Did you really think I was going to tell you I was carrying your child? After you'd thrown me out of your life like I was yesterday's used tissue? Paying me off like a *whore*!'

His face darkened. 'God almighty, would you have thought better of me if I'd just ended it flat, without even saying thank you to you?'

She yanked her hands free, jerking back with all her effort.

'You didn't have to *thank* me for the sex. Dear God, I knew I was a fool to go anywhere near you, but I didn't think—I didn't think it was going to…going to…going to—'

She choked off. 'Oh, God, what's the use? I know what you are—I've known for four years. And last night I found out all over again. Didn't I? *Didn't I?* You were feeling randy and there was no one else around—so why not take whatever was on hand? Even if it did risk another unplanned pregnancy. You wanted some instant sex, and you took it. And don't throw back at me that I didn't say no. Because I *know* what a criminal fool I was last night. What an unforgivable idiot! Just like I was four years ago. A complete fool to go and fall in lo—'

She broke off, horrified, dismayed, wanting the ground to swallow her. She stumbled to her feet, staggering away, her eyes still blind with tears, her throat still tearing, lungs heaving. Tears were pouring down her cheeks, into her mouth, her nose was running and her face was hurting.

He caught at her hand, bolting to his feet to seize at her. She threw him off, heading blindly to the sea. She had to escape—she *had* to! How could she have said that? Just blurted it out like that? How could she?

Behind her, Xander stood stock still.

Completely motionless.

Yet inside him, like a very slow explosion, her words were detonating through him.

What had she just said?

Slowly, like a dead man walking, he followed her.

She was standing, feet in the water, her back to him. Her shoulders were still heaving, and he could still hear ragged, tearing sobs, quieter now.

With a more desperate, despairing sound.

He noticed little things about her.

Her pigtail was ragged, frazzling at the end. The sun glinted on the pale gold of her hair. Her waist was very narrow—he could almost have spanned it with his hand. Her legs were tanned.

So many things—so many things he noticed.

He knew her body—knew it from memory, and from this week he'd spent watching her, letting his desire for her grow day by day to suit his purpose, his dark, malign purpose.

Last night he had possessed her body, known it intimately. As he had four years ago.

But he hadn't known her.

He hadn't known her at all.

Slowly, very slowly, he spoke.

'What did you just say?'

She started. Had she not heard him approach on the soft sand?

'What did you just say, Clare?' he said again.

Her shoulders hunched. When she spoke, her voice was shaky, raking.

'I said I hated you. I said I loathed you. And if I didn't, I should have. And I'll say it now instead.'

He shook his head. She couldn't see the gesture, but he didn't care. It came automatically to him.

'But that isn't true, is it, Clare? That's not true at all. Not four years ago when you sat at that table in the St John and I told you it was over. You didn't hate me then. It wasn't hate, was it, Clare? Not then.'

His hands curved over her shoulders. He turned her around to him. The sunlight blinded her eyes. Or something did. She stood looking at him. Hollowed out, emptied out.

'I hated you,' she whispered. 'You threw me out of your life. I hated you.'

He shook his head. Sunlight glanced on the sable of his hair. She felt faintness draining through her, her legs too weak to stand. He held her steady by her shoulders. His hands were warm and strong, pressing into her through her T-shirt.

'You didn't, Clare. You didn't hate me then. You didn't hate me at all.'

'Yes, I did. I did and I do!' Her voice was fierce, so fierce.

His thumbs rubbed on her collarbone, slow and strange.

'You gave yourself away, Clare. Just now. Gave yourself away. For the first time. The only time. Gave yourself clean away. And now I know, don't I? I know why you walked away from me never to return, not even for your clothes, your books, your toothbrush—everything you left at my apartment.'

'You should be *grateful* that I did. Grateful.' The fierceness was still in her voice, raw and rasping. 'I must have been the easiest mistress to dump you'd ever had.'

His face stilled. There was something very strange in his eyes. Very strange indeed. She couldn't tell what it was. It must be the sun blinding her. That was all it could be...

For a long, endless moment he was silent. She felt the gentle lap of water round her feet. Felt the hot sun beating down on her. Felt his hands over her shoulders, pressing down on her. They were completely still—like him.

Then, into the silence, he spoke.

'You were the hardest,' he said.

Her eyes flared. 'The hardest?' she jeered bitterly. 'You said

"It's over" and I *went*! I went without a question, without a word! I just *went*!"

'You were the hardest,' he said again.

He dropped his hands from her. She felt bereft.

His face was sombre.

'I got rid of you because I had to. To save my sanity. To keep me safe. Because I was scared—in the biggest danger I'd ever been in. And I couldn't hack it.' His jaw tightened. 'When I went to New York that last time I knew I had to act. I knew I could put it off no longer. Because the danger was—terrifying. And I knew when I came back that I had to deal with it. Fast. Urgently. Permanently.'

His eyes rested on her. They had no expression in them. She had seen them look that way before…

'So I did. I dealt with it. Immediately. Ruthlessly. Brutally.'

He paused again. 'And it worked. Worked so perfectly. But as I realised that you had simply…gone…I realised something else as well.'

His eyes were still on her. Expressionless eyes. Except for one faint, impossible fragment…

'I realised,' he said, and each word fell from him like a weight, 'I would have given anything in the world to have you back.'

His eyes moved past her. Out to the sea beyond. A sea without limits. Without a horizon.

'But you were gone. As if I'd pressed a button. Just…gone. I started to look for you, to wait for you. You had to come back— you'd left everything with me. So you *had* to come back. But you never did. You just—vanished.'

'You said I did it to try and make you come after me.' Her voice was still very faint.

He kept looking out to sea, far out to sea. As if into the past.

'I wanted it to be for that reason. I wanted it to be for *any* reason that meant that you didn't *want* to go. That you wanted to come back to me—that you wanted me to come after you.' He breathed in harshly, spoke harshly. 'That you *did* feel something for me. Then—when finally I'd accepted that when I'd said "It's over" to you, you had indeed gone for ever—then…' His eyes went to her, hard, unforgiving. 'I told myself that I had made the right decision after all—that there was no point regretting it, no point wishing I had not done what I had. You'd felt nothing for me. Nothing at all. Which meant I had to move on, get over it. Get on with my life. So that's what I did. I had no choice—you were gone. So I got on with my life.'

She shut her eyes, then opened them again.

'You were angry with me when you saw me again.'

The sombre look was in his eyes again.

'I was angry with you because you'd been able to walk away from me without a second glance. With nothing—nothing at all. I was angry with you because you'd made me live with the choice I'd made. The decision I'd made. To play safe. And by playing safe to lose what I most wanted.'

He took another harsh breath. 'You. That's what I wanted. *You.*'

She looked into his eyes. 'Why?' It was all she said—all she could say.

Something moved in his eyes.

'Why?' His voice changed. *'Why?'* he echoed. 'Because I wanted you there, still. With me. Not to let you go.' He looked at her again. 'It scared me. I'd never wanted that before. Never. Not with any woman. Not even with you until I realised, that last time we had together, before I went to New York, that you had become important to me. And it scared me—scared me sense-less—because I had never felt anything like that before, because it made me feel afraid and out of control—and worst, worst of all, it made me realise that I had no idea, *none*, of what you felt.'

He looked at her.

'You never showed your emotions to me, Clare. You were always so reserved. I couldn't read you—I didn't know what you felt, if you felt anything at all. That scared me even more. So I wanted out. Because that was the safest call to make.'

His eyes slipped past her again.

'I was a fool,' he said heavily. 'I made the wrong call. And because of that I lost you. And I lost the son you were carrying. The son you hid from me. And now I know why—I know why you never told me about Joey.'

His gaze shot to her again, holding her like rods of fire. 'I know why, and the knowledge kills me. And it hurts me to think what I did to you last night. Do you know why I did it, Clare—do you?'

His hands had come up again, to lie heavy on her shoulders. 'I deliberately, cold-bloodedly took you to bed last night with one purpose only—to get you pregnant. I *had* to get you pregnant! I had to. Because if you were pregnant again, then this time, *this time*, you would have to marry me. You couldn't turn me down. I'd make sure of it. And that way I'd get Joey—I'd get Joey, and he's all I wanted. When I discovered you'd hidden my son from me, the only reason I could come up with for why you'd done it was to punish me for finishing with you. The reaction of a woman scorned. And it vindicated me. Vindicated what I'd done to you, the call I'd made. A woman who could vengefully hide my son from me wasn't a woman I wanted in my life, wasn't a woman I should…care about. But that wasn't why you hid Joey from me, was it, Clare? *Was it?*'

'No.' It was a whisper. All she could manage.

'It was because I hurt you,' he said. 'I hurt you so badly that night at the St John that all you could do was walk. Run. Hide. For ever. And there was only one reason why I could have hurt you.'

His hands slid from her shoulders, cupping her face, lifting it to his so that she had to look deep, deep into his eyes.

'Why was I able to hurt you, Clare? Hurt you so badly?' His voice was strained. Desperate. 'Please tell me—please. I don't deserve it—but—'

'I was in love with you,' she said.

For one long, agonising moment there was silence. Then, 'Thank God,' he said. 'Thank God.'

His thumbs smoothed along her cheekbones. Silent tears were running.

'Don't cry, Clare. Don't ever cry for me again. I'll never let you cry again. Not for me. Not ever for me.'

He gazed down into her swimming eyes. 'I'm going to do everything in my power, Clare, to win that love again. Everything. Because, fool that I was—that I am—fool that I have been in everything to do with you—I at least now know this. I had fallen in love with you then, four years ago, and didn't realize—refused to believe I was capable of it And I still love you. I know that completely and absolutely, because last night—' he gave a shuddering breath '—last night was my own punishment. My punishment for having denied what I felt for you—a terrible punishment. Because last night I realised, with all the horror in the world, that I still love you—love a woman who had felt nothing for me, had been able to walk away from me without a word, who had wreaked vindictive revenge on me for having spurned her by keeping my own son from me.

'But it was never, *never* that that stopped you telling me about Joey. It was because you could not bear to have anything to do with the man who had hurt you—because you love me.' His voice changed, and she could hear the pain in it. 'I've wronged you so much, Clare. Four years ago I hurt you unbearably—and I've hurt you again. I can't ask for your love again, but I will win it back—with all my being. Ah, no, don't weep, Clare—not for me, never for me!' His thumbs smoothed again, but her eyes were spilling, spilling uncontrollably, and her face was crumpling, and she couldn't stop, couldn't stop.

He wrapped her to him. And the feel of his arms going about her, holding her so close, so safe, was the most wonderful feeling in all the world, all there could ever be. He held her so tightly, as if he would never, *could* never let her go. She could hear words, murmuring, soothing, and she could not understand them, but it did not matter.

She could hear them in her heart. Know them in her heart.

And it was all she needed. All she would ever need.

Slowly, holding her hand, Xander walked her back towards the villa.

'I didn't know anything about love. Did not know that that was what I had started to feel for you. I only knew that you were a woman I did not want to lose. A woman whose cool composure seemed to inflame me with desire.'

A sensual, reminiscent smile played at his mouth, and Clare felt the so-familiar weakness start inside her.

'It got to me—every time. More and more. I revelled in the

difference that only I could make in you, the sensuality beneath the surface that only I could release in you. When we were out together I didn't like you to touch me. I liked you to look un-touched—untouchable. Waiting for me. Waiting for me to get you back to the hotel, the apartment, where I could finally indulge myself in doing what I'd been holding back from all evening…'

Clare looked at him. Was that why he had been like that? Not because he'd thought her out of line being physically demonstrative towards him even in the briefest way?

'I didn't know,' she said. Her voice was faint again.

He glanced at her, frowning. 'You must have known—I couldn't keep my hands off you. You must have seen that I was…losing control. And that last time—surely that last time you must have seen, known, sensed that I was…?'

Her throat tightened. Pain, remembered pain, pierced her.

'I did! I thought it meant—meant that you were begin-ning…that I might mean something to you. But then…' she could hardly speak '…then you came back and took me out to dinner, and I was trying to screw up my courage, to pin my hopes on a future with you and tell you…tell you that I was pregnant.' She swallowed. 'And then you spoke first.'

His hand crushed hers, tightening automatically. He stopped dead.

'*Theos mou*—that it should have hung in the balance on so fine a thread. How the gods mocked me that night. If I had only—only—'

Anguish silenced him. She lifted his hand with hers, bringing it to her mouth and kissing it as she might Joey's, to comfort him.

'We can't undo the past, Xander—neither of us can. We can only—' her voice caught '—only be grateful—so very, very grateful—that we have been given a second chance.' She took a deep, painful breath. 'I know I should have come back to tell you about Joey. I know that. I've known it all these years, and fought it. Fought it for my own selfish reasons. Because I was too much a coward to think of anyone but myself. Because I could not face letting you back into my life after you had thrown me out of it. Could not face being what I knew I must be—the unwanted mother of your son. I told myself I did not need to tell you because you would not want Joey anyway—that you would, out of common decency, pay for him, but you would not want him. And when you found out about him, and you were so angry, I knew—I knew you had a right to be. But I didn't want to admit it—to face up to it!'

She took another unforgiving breath.

'I've been punished for keeping him from you—not just by your anger, but by my shame at keeping him from you, not giving you the chance to say you wanted him, not giving Joey what I knew he could have had. A father. And by more—by the knowledge that if I'd just gone back to you, if I hadn't in my pride, my own pain and anger, kept away from you...'

'It would have been a reward I did not deserve,' Xander said heavily, condemningly. 'Not after my cowardice in not admitting to myself what I had come to feel for you, in denying my own emotions. Not after my cruelty in the way I ended it—so brutally, so unfeelingly. Even if you had not loved me it would still have been brutal. But knowing now what you were feeling as I sat there and said those words to you—' He broke off, pain in his eyes.

Clare's heart filled. 'It's over, Xander. It's gone. Don't torment yourself. Let's start again—a clean slate, a new beginning.' She paused, her eyes lambent suddenly. 'Did you mean it—about last night? That you were trying get me pregnant?'

His face shadowed instantly. '*Theos mou*, Clare—forgive me for that. I should never have—'

'But I don't forgive you,' she said. 'I *thank* you! Oh, Xander, can we have another child? Now?'

Xander caught her and swept her up into his arms. She gave a gasp, and clutched her arms around his neck.

'Joey can have a dozen brothers and sisters. And I, my most adored one, will take the greatest, most grateful pleasure in fathering each and every one of them.'

His mouth caught hers, warm and soft and so full of love that it was like heaven in her heart. She felt her body quicken, answering with swift eagerness the arousal of his touch as he carried her off, bearing her away, striding swiftly over the grass to reach the terrace, sliding back the bedroom door with a powerful glide of his arm.

Inside, the instant cool of the room embraced them—but it could not quench the heat rising between them, the heat of passion, of desire, as they came down on the bed in a sweet tangle of limbs.

'I love you so much,' he said, gazing down into her eyes. 'I loved you then; I love you now. I will love you for ever. I love everything about you. Everything that is you. *Everything*. Except—' his expression changed suddenly, and there was a disapproving frown on his face '—this.'

He lifted the long frayed end of her pigtail and eyed it with critical disdain.

'This has to go,' he told her. 'No negotiation.'

'It's very practical,' said Clare.

'You don't need practical,' he said. 'You just need me. And I—' his fingers deftly disposed of the restraining band and then started to unplait the strands, '—just need you. And we both—' he flicked free her hair, running his fingers through the pale gold of it '—need Joey, and Joey needs us—and a new brother or sister!'

She pulled his head down to her and kissed him. Then she pushed his head back a little, so she could speak.

'Xander,' she told him, 'Joey has been with Juliette for a good long time now, and soon he's going to have finished hosing down the cars, and anyone else within range, and realise that he hasn't been swimming yet. And that means he's going to want you to take him. And *that* means—' she pulled him down to kiss him again, then let him go to finish speaking '—we had really, *really* better get on with this! Right now.'

'Oh, Kyria Xander Anaketos-to-be…' Xander's voice husked, his eyes agleam with anticipation. 'How very, *very* happy I am to oblige.'

His mouth lowered to hers, and softly, sensuously, with tenderness and desire, passion and pleasure, he began to make love to her.

EPILOGUE

THE sun was setting over the Aegean in a splendour of gold. Enthroned in a huge bath chair on the foredeck, and adorned with a very extravagant hat, Vi surveyed the scene, a satisfied smile on her wrinkled face. But it was not the gold and crimson sky that drew her approbation. It was the sight of Clare and Xander, still in their wedding finery, their arms around each other's waists, gazing out over the sea through which the huge yacht was carving its smooth path.

On her lap sat Joey, resplendent in a tuxedo the miniature version of his father's.

'Tell me a story, Nan,' said Joey.

Vi settled her shoulders into the cushions and reached for the cup of tea that wasn't quite as good as proper English tea, seeing how it had been made by a Greek chef, but was very welcome for all that. It had been a long day for her, but one that had brought a lift to her heart. Young people really could be so foolish, so blind and so stubborn—it took such a lot to make them see sense.

'A story?' she said, and took a mouthful of tea before setting down the cup carefully. Her eyes went to the couple by the rail, who had turned to each other. 'Well, let's see. Once upon a time there was a princess, and a prince fell in love with her, but he was very silly and didn't say so. And the Princess fell in love with him, and *she* was very silly and didn't say so. And so they parted. And the Princess had a baby, but she was even sillier then, and didn't tell the Prince, and so—'

Joey was tugging her sleeve. Vi turned from watching his parents gazing into each other's eyes.

'What is it, pet?' she asked.

There was a disgusted look on his face. 'Nan, tell me a *proper* story. With knights in armour. And dragons. And fast cars.'

He snuggled back against her. Vi took another sip of tea. 'Oh, a *proper* story? Well, let's see…'

She started to weave a story with the elements her charge required.

At the prow of the yacht, Xander was lowering his head to Clare, and she was lifting her face to his. The setting sun turned their kiss to gold, and Vi paused in her tale, wiping a tear from her eye. Yes, the young were foolish, blind, and stubborn—but they got there in the end.

And that was all that mattered.

* * * * *

THE MILLIONAIRE'S CONTRACT BRIDE

Carole Mortimer

CHAPTER ONE

'WHAT on earth are you doing here?' Casey gasped. She had arrived home exhausted at almost eleven o'clock after working that evening, only to come to a shocked halt in the doorway to her sitting room and stare at the man sitting there so unconcernedly.

The single source of light in the room came from a small table lamp, casting the man's face in shadow as he sat in the armchair across the room. But even though she had only met him twice—briefly—in her life before, it was still possible for Casey to recognise the dark overlong hair, the wide shoulders and the tall, leanly powerful frame as belonging to Xander Fraser—a man whose brooding good-looks often graced the more prestigious gossip magazines as he attended the premieres of the numerous films released by his production company.

A man she hadn't realised even knew where she lived.

Yes, they both lived in Surrey, but at completely different ends of the housing scale. The Fraser mansion was set in several wooded acres of grounds near the river, while her own home was on an estate and much, much smaller.

If she hadn't been so shocked at finding him here, she might even have found a certain pleasure in having this ruggedly handsome man in her home. After all, he was the first eligible, gorgeous man she had been this close to since her marriage had ended a year ago.

Or perhaps not, she acknowledged with an inward grimace; she was hardly looking her best at the moment. Her hair probably smelt of the food cooked at the restaurant this evening, she was wearing some of her oldest clothes—for the same reason—and wore absolutely no make-up whatsoever to add colour to her naturally pale complexion.

Besides which, it was hardly a good idea for her to be attracted to the ex-husband of the woman who had stolen her own husband!

Xander Fraser shrugged those broad shoulders, shifting slightly so that his face was no longer in shadow, revealing an aquiline nose between high cheekbones, and an arrogant slash of a mouth above a strongly squared chin. He regarded her with hooded blue eyes. 'I was waiting for you to get home, obviously,' he drawled.

'Yes, I realise that,' she answered impatiently; it was why he was here that was important! 'But—where's Hannah?' she asked, her voice sharpening with alarm.

Now that her first shock on seeing Xander was receding, Casey realised the girl she employed to look after her son on the evenings she worked at the restaurant was noticeably absent.

'Is that the name of the babysitter?' Xander Fraser quirked dark brows. 'I told her she might as well take advantage of my being here and go home early.'

'And she just went?' Casey exclaimed. 'But she doesn't even know you! You could have been anybody!'

'Such as?' Those dark brows rose a second time. 'A mass-murderer? Or a kidnapper, perhaps?' He gave a humourless smile.

'Well…actually, yes,' Casey said with a frown, feeling she had every right to be annoyed with Hannah's irresponsible behaviour.

Although Xander Fraser hardly looked the part of either, she acknowledged privately to herself, dressed in those designer label denims and navy blue silk shirt, and possessed of the kind of confidence that only the very rich or very good-looking seemed to acquire.

Xander Fraser scowled. 'Believe me, the complications that go along with the one child I have are more than enough for me to cope with right now!'

His daughter Lauren was six years old—the same age as Casey's son Josh. But there the similarities ended. Lauren Fraser was the daughter of multimillionaire film producer Xander Fraser, whereas Josh was the son of a single mother juggling two jobs to try and keep a roof over their heads.

She sighed as she put her handbag down on the coffee table, too tired to be able to make much sense out of this man's unexpected presence here, let alone his enigmatic conversation.

It had been a long day for her. She'd got up at seven-thirty, to get her young son ready and at school for nine o'clock, then hurried off to the café she worked in until after the lunchtime rush. Once that was over, she'd collected Josh and spent a couple of hours at home with him, before leaving for her evening job at the restaurant of the local hotel.

Yes, it had been a very long and very tiring day, and she was in no mood to play verbal fencing games with Xander Fraser, of all people. Whether he was sinfully handsome or not!

As he was sitting in the only chair in her sparsely furnished sitting room, Casey remained standing, still very unhappy with Hannah—but that, she promised herself, was something she would take up with the girl tomorrow.

'So, what can I do for you, Mr Fraser?' she challenged tersely.

With her painfully thin frame clothed in a figure-hugging black tee shirt and faded blue denims, and at only a couple of inches over five feet tall, Casey Bridges had all the appearance of a bantam hen aligning itself against a hawk, Xander decided ruefully. Her soft blonde hair was styled wispily about her temples and nape, and her beautiful heart-shaped face was dominated by dark green eyes that did absolutely nothing to dispel that illusion of fragility.

And she looked exhausted... Even as he thought it, she swayed slightly on her feet.

Abruptly, Xander stood up. 'Sit down,' he commanded, 'before you collapse.'

She obviously bridled at the order, but then did as he'd said. Perhaps she realised he was fully capable of picking her up and sitting her in the chair himself, if she refused...

The chair, the coffee table and the lamp were the only furniture in the room. He had noted that with a frown when he'd arrived earlier. There was no television in the room, either, and when he had taken a quick look around the rest of the house he had found that to be no better. Casey Bridges seemed to have taken the 'minimalist' effect to a barren degree.

Or else—as his daughter Lauren had already hinted—there was another explanation altogether for such austerity...

Xander's eyes narrowed as he registered just how fragilely thin the woman before him was. He noted the shadows beneath those dark green eyes, the hollows beneath her cheekbones, and the skin on her hands and wrists that was almost translucent.

'Exactly what's been going on here, Casey?' he asked, his blue gaze uncomfortably penetrating now. 'Where were you this evening?' He had thought she must be out with friends—possibly even a boyfriend, as her husband had left her a year ago—but she hardly had the look of a woman returning from a pleasant evening out.

She gave a firm shake of her head as she seemed to regain some of her composure. 'That really isn't any of your business, Mr Fraser.' She stood up. 'I should go up and check on Josh. I still can't believe— Has he woken up? Is he aware that Hannah has left?' she asked anxiously.

'Josh is fine,' Xander assured her. 'He did wake up once, but when I told him I was Lauren's daddy he wasn't concerned. He and Lauren have become friends—did you know that?'

Yes, she did know that. Ironically, Josh and Lauren had become friends during the eight months when Sam and Chloe had lived together, their visits to their individual parents often coinciding. Casey also knew that Josh had missed seeing the little girl since Chloe and Sam's deaths four months ago.

'Yes, I believe they have—did,' she corrected. 'If you would just like to wait here while I go and check on Josh, we can—continue this conversation when I come back down.' Her gaze didn't quite meet his before she turned and left the room, to run up the stairs to Josh's small bedroom above with a vague feeling of relief.

She had to admit to finding Xander Fraser's powerful presence and fiercely intelligent blue eyes slightly overwhelming in the small confines of the three-bedroomed house that she had lived in first with her parents, then with Sam and Josh, and now just with Josh. The house she was determined to hold on to if humanly possible.

Quite what sort of conversation she and Xander Fraser were going to have she had no idea, but he obviously considered it important enough for him to have gone to the trouble of finding out where she lived.

She very much doubted Xander's ex-wife would have told him. Casey and Xander's previous two meetings had been when they'd happened to call at the same time to collect Josh and Lauren after one of their weekend visits to the house Sam and Chloe had so briefly shared. The dazzlingly beautiful Chloe had had no choice but to introduce the two of them, but her hypnotic blue eyes had been narrowed on them watchfully as she'd done so.

Casey hadn't liked the sophisticated but brittle Chloe Fraser; she knew she wouldn't have liked her even if she hadn't been 'the other woman' in Casey's marriage break-up. The two of them had absolutely nothing in common—except Sam, of course.

Only Chloe Fraser's beauty had been such that her more negative traits obviously hadn't repulsed the golden and handsome Sam, or the darkly brooding and immensely rich Xander Fraser.

But the fact that Chloe and Sam were now both dead—killed four months ago when the private jet they'd been travelling in had crashed—meant that Josh and Lauren's visits to them had obviously stopped, too. And it should have meant that Casey would never have reason to see Xander Fraser again, either.

So why on earth was he downstairs in her sitting room, obviously waiting to talk to her?

CHAPTER TWO

XANDER became aware of Casey's presence behind him as he stood in the kitchen. 'You looked like you could do with a cup,' he explained, as he turned and saw her brows raised at the two steaming mugs of coffee he had just made. 'How was Josh?' he prompted, when he noted the pallor of those hollow cheeks.

The shadows remained in her deep green eyes but she smiled. Deep grooves appeared beside the fullness of her lips, as if humour was something that hadn't come easily to her recently.

And Xander doubted that it had. To Chloe, he knew, the seduction of the man who had come to their home as a landscape gardener had all been a game. A game she had played more times than even Xander was aware of. Or cared about. Although in Sam Bridges' case Chloe had very quickly decided that she wanted to take their relationship to the next level—so the two of them had left their partners and set up home together.

The fact that at the same time she had robbed this woman of her husband, and six-year-old Josh of his father, wouldn't have been of interest to the spoilt and wilful Chloe. She had seen something she wanted, and taken it without hesitation.

'Fast asleep,' Casey acknowledged ruefully. Then she flushed slightly. 'Er—would you like a biscuit or something to go with that coffee?'

As he had checked all the cupboards in the kitchen while she was upstairs, and found them all bare—just like Old Mother

Hubbard's in the nursery rhyme—Xander didn't hold out much hope of there being anything for him to actually have.

'No, thanks—I ate earlier,' he said easily. 'Shall we go through to the sitting room, or would you prefer to stand in here and talk?' Either way, only one of them would be able to sit!

Once again Xander wondered what the hell had been going on in this woman's life these last four months. There was no food in the house, and very little furniture, either, and Casey Bridges looked as if a strong gust of wind would knock her off her feet.

'Here is fine.' Casey took one of the steaming mugs of coffee from him, her hand carefully avoiding coming into contact with his as she did so.

It was ridiculous, she told herself impatiently, to be so aware of this man. So physically aware of him. But there was no denying that her hands were trembling slightly with that awareness.

Perhaps she was just missing having sex?

Surely not! The physical side of her marriage to Sam hadn't been that good in the first place, and had been completely non-existent for the last six months they'd been together. No, it had to be Xander Fraser himself who had awakened all these sensual longings within her...

Her mouth tightened at the knowledge. 'What did you want to talk to me about—?'

'That can wait,' he cut in abruptly. 'First I would like you to tell me why there's hardly any furniture in the house, and why the fridge is also bare, except for a bottle of milk and a piece of cheese.'

Her eyes widened with incredulous anger. 'You've been looking through my refrigerator?'

'I needed milk for your coffee,' he pointed out with a sardonic smile. His own coffee was black.

'Oh.' Casey felt her cheeks warm at the rebuke. 'But, still, what I do or don't have in my refrigerator is none of your concern—'

'When did you last eat, Casey?' Xander Fraser asked bluntly, ignoring her attempt to put him in his place.

'I don't have to—'

'Yes, you do,' he interrupted again, his tone brooking no more denial or evasions.

She frowned her deep irritation at his autocratic attitude.

'I cooked lamb chops, new potatoes and vegetables for tea before I went out—'

'I'm prepared to accept that *Josh* had lamb chops and vegetables for his evening meal. Unlike you, he looks robustly healthy,' he added pointedly. 'Besides, I saw the bones from two chops in your pedal bin just now—'

'Mr Fraser, you really do *not* have the right to question me like this!' Casey gasped. 'Let alone go poking around in my pedal bin!' she added indignantly.

No, he probably didn't, Xander acknowledged grimly. And he really couldn't say that he had given this woman, or her son, much consideration during the last year, either. He had been too busy for most of that time trying to deal with the trauma that Chloe's desertion and subsequent death had caused his own daughter to worry about Sam Bridges' family.

But all that had changed since his conversation with Brad Henderson, Chloe's father, four days ago…

Since arriving at Casey's home a couple of hours ago, and seeing the frugal way she lived, Xander was inclined to think the claim Lauren had made once that 'Josh's mummy is so poor she can't buy him any new toys' was probably a true one. Not that it gave Xander any pleasure to know that; it just meant, as he had hoped, that Casey might be the answer to his own dilemma.

In fact, if Casey were willing to be co-operative and agree to what he was about to suggest, she would be vastly improving her own situation at the same time as she helped Xander turn this whole situation around on Brad Henderson.

If Casey were willing to be co-operative…

Looking at her now, he could see just how completely exhausted she was—both physically and emotionally. He didn't think that it was all due to the trauma of the events of the past year alone; from the little Xander had bothered to learn about Sam Bridges, the man hadn't exactly been the perfect husband and provider for his family even before he'd become involved with Chloe.

No wonder his ex-wife had been so drawn to the man. They'd been two of a kind. Spoilt users, the pair of them.

Xander shrugged unapologetically. 'Perhaps if you stop treating me like an idiot and answer my questions honestly I might stop poking my nose into your pedal bin and your business.' Despite the mildness of his tone, he was nevertheless determined to have answers to his questions. 'Where were you this evening, Casey?' He was pretty sure now that she hadn't been out for an evening of frivolity—the woman didn't look as if she even knew the meaning of the word.

Casey looked up at him in a slight daze, still having no idea what had prompted this man's visit, or why he was questioning her so intently. She was only aware that she was simply too tired to argue with him any longer…

'I was at work,' she sighed. 'I work four evenings a week in the restaurant of a local hotel.'

Xander Fraser scowled darkly. 'Wouldn't it have been more convenient, with Josh still so young, for you to have found a job in the day—?'

'I *do* have a job in the day!' she told him impatiently, feeling at a distinct disadvantage as his body, with its superior height, loomed over hers; Xander Fraser was at least a foot taller than her own five feet two inches. 'I work five days a week cooking at a local café as well as the four evenings at the hotel,' she revealed, still reluctant to discuss her personal business with this man who exuded such wealth and power.

'Why?' he probed.

Her cheeks flushed. 'That is none of your—'

'Business?' Xander finished for her. 'What if I'm *making* it my business?' he added softly, becoming more and more convinced as he talked to Casey that he had found the answer to getting out of the corner Brad was pushing him into.

That what he was about to propose would solve Casey's problems, too…

She gave a disbelieving laugh, at once looking younger, even if the expression in her green eyes was derisive rather than genuinely amused. 'And why would Xander Fraser, multimillionaire film producer, want to do something like that?' she scorned, highlighting the immense gulf between their vastly different circumstances.

Not that she wanted to be mega-rich. Comfortably off would be nice. But the garden centre and the money that her father had left her when he died were long gone—the first bankrupted in a year under Sam's management, the second frittered away as he had struggled to make a success—played at?—landscape gardening.

The only thing Sam had succeeded at was ending their torturous marriage once and for all by meeting Chloe Fraser!

'Well, Mr Fraser?' she said belligerently.

His mouth thinned at her tone of voice. 'I have—a business proposition to put to you,' he finally bit out.

Casey shook her head. 'I'm afraid you've misunderstood my cooking abilities, Mr Fraser. I don't cater for dinner parties—'

'Not that sort of business proposition!' he growled, pacing the small confines of the kitchen, his gaze narrowed to vivid blue slits. 'Are you familiar with Brad Henderson?'

Her eyebrows raised at the mention of the rich, retired owner of a Hollywood film studio. 'Not personally, no.'

'I am,' Xander said.

Casey shrugged. 'You're both in the same business.'

'He's also Chloe's father,' Xander expanded. 'And therefore Lauren's grandfather.'

Casey hadn't known that—although it probably went a long way towards explaining why Chloe had always been so sure of having her own way. A privileged, over-indulgent father, followed by marriage to an even richer husband—what choice had the other woman had but to be spoilt and selfish?

All of which was of absolutely no relevance whatsoever now that Chloe was dead.

Was it…?

Casey put up a tired hand to brush her hair away from her brow. 'I really don't see what this has to do with me.'

'I'm getting to that,' Xander assured her impatiently. 'Lauren and Josh are already friends. Things obviously aren't going too well with you if you have to work at two jobs in order to remain even this financially solvent—'

'Now, look, Mr Fraser—'

'Will you just hear me out, Casey?' Xander cut in. 'I have

something to say, and your constant interruptions aren't making it any easier!'

She raised blonde brows, indignant colour in her cheeks. 'Maybe if you stopped making this so personal...?'

His mouth twisted humourlessly. 'But it *is* personal, Casey. Very personal,' he added heavily. 'For reasons that I will explain in a moment, I'm here to ask if, in return for my financially providing for you and Josh, you would consider becoming my wife.'

Speechless.

Xander Fraser had rendered her completely speechless with his announcement—his question?

He couldn't possibly be serious!

Could he?

CHAPTER THREE

CASEY felt as if she were fighting her way through cotton-wool—thick, wispy clouds of it that stopped her reaching the surface, stopped her from remembering—

This was all a dream! Xander Fraser was a dream. As his marriage proposal had been a dream—

'Drink this,' rasped an autocratic voice. 'Come on, Casey, open your eyes and drink.'

Unfortunately, that voice was all too familiar. Not a dream, then. Or even a nightmare! Which meant that Xander's marriage proposal had been very real...

'I know you're awake, Casey.' His voice was softer now. 'I'm not going to disappear just because you refuse to open your eyes and look at me,' he taunted gently.

Her lids snapped open and she glared up at her tormentor. She was now sitting slumped in the armchair Xander must have carried her to when she'd fainted, and he was bent over her, holding out a glass of clear brown liquid.

A rueful smile touched those beautifully sculpted lips as he made no effort to back off. 'Drink some of the sherry, Casey,' he ordered as he held the glass closer to her. 'It should be brandy, I know, but it's all I could find in the way of alcohol,' he added wryly.

It was cooking sherry, Casey recognised with a grimace as she took the glass from him, used to flavour a trifle she had made for Christmas, several months ago. And not a very good cooking sherry, either. But he was right. She needed something to dispel some of the numbed shock she was feeling.

Xander Fraser was the type of man who was always right, she decided, thoroughly disgruntled. She gulped down the sherry, finding it as disgusting as she'd thought it would be, but nonetheless reviving for all that.

Great, Xander muttered inwardly when he saw those green eyes begin to sparkle unnaturally and the flush that suddenly coloured Casey's previously pale cheeks; one glass of bloody awful sherry and the woman was drunk. No doubt the fact that she obviously didn't eat properly hadn't helped.

'That's enough of that,' he said firmly. He took the empty glass away from her and placed it on the coffee table, straightening as he did so to move slightly away from her. His deliberately bland expression showed none of the concern he had felt a few minutes ago, as he'd carried her limp body from the kitchen to place her in the chair in the sitting room.

The woman had been like gossamer in his arms—so light she'd felt as though she didn't weigh much more than Lauren. As he had looked down at her he'd wondered what difference a few good meals and some TLC would bring to the hollows of her cheeks and the slender curves of her body. How she would look if the worry and stress she was obviously suffering were to be removed and she could actually start to enjoy life again.

Then he had chastised himself for even thinking along those lines. His idea that the two of them marry was a business proposition. Nothing more, nothing less. Far better that he didn't even think of Casey Bridges' undoubted beauty, or the possible allure of her with a fuller, more curvaceous body...

No, thinking about her like that certainly wasn't a good idea. Not if she agreed to marry him.

And he had every intention, now he had actually voiced the idea, of making sure that she did!

Casey looked up at Xander from beneath long golden lashes, easily recognising his leashed strength as he paced the room restlessly. He was a man who wielded power along with supreme self-confidence. A man, she was sure, who never took no for an answer. A man who had just suggested, with the offer of a financial incentive, that she marry him!

She moistened stiff, unyielding lips before speaking. 'I think you had better leave now.'

'I'm afraid I can't do that, Casey. You and I have a lot more to say to each other before I agree to go anywhere.'

'But you can't have seriously just suggested the two of us get *married?*'

'Oh, I'm serious,' he replied grimly. 'Very much so.'

'But you don't even know me—'

'I know all I need to know,' he declared. 'You're hardworking. Independent. A good mother—'

'My teeth are sound, too,' she put in sarcastically.

Xander gave an appreciative grin. 'There—you have a sense of humour as well!'

'It's hysteria, Mr Fraser, not humour,' Casey pointed out, sitting up straighter in the armchair to look at him searchingly. 'Why?' she finally voiced in a guarded tone.

'Add *astute* to your list of attributes!' he teased, not unkindly.

'Well, I certainly know you aren't suggesting I marry you because you've suddenly decided you've fallen madly in love with me!' she retorted.

'No,' he acknowledged seriously. 'Do you want to know why you? Or why I need to get married at all?'

'Both,' Casey snapped.

'Does Josh have any paternal grandparents?' he asked, instead of answering either of those questions.

Casey looked surprised. 'Yes.'

'And have they ever considered trying to take Josh from you?'

'After the way their son behaved? They wouldn't dare!' she assured him, wings of angry colour appearing in those pale cheeks.

'Well, Brad feels no such scruples where his granddaughter is concerned,' Xander said coldly.

'Your father-in-law wants to take Lauren away from you?' Casey gasped. 'But why?'

Xander raised an eyebrow. 'Why does he want Lauren? Or why does he think he has reason to take Lauren from me?'

'Either. Both!' Casey frowned her agitation at his habit of answering her questions with more questions, at the same time wondering how she would have felt if Sam's parents had ever threatened to try and take Josh from her.

As desperate as Xander Fraser obviously did, if his marriage proposal to her was anything to go by!

He sighed. 'Brad is hurting very badly at the moment. His daughter—his only child—died four months ago, and now that his initial shock has receded I believe he sees Lauren as a replacement in his life for Chloe. He informed me on Sunday that he intends applying for custody of Lauren. I tried reasoning with him, and pointed out that he isn't thinking rationally at the moment. He isn't listening,' Xander concluded darkly.

Casey gave him a searching look, knowing by the grimness of his expression that he took his father-in-law's threat seriously. But surely Brad Henderson, no matter how rich and influential, could never succeed in such a threat?

'You didn't answer my other *why*,' she prompted.

Xander Fraser's eyes flashed. 'Why does he think he might succeed in such a claim?' His lips briefly compressed into a tight line before he continued. 'Whether you believe me or not, I consider myself a good father. But there have been—problems since Chloe and I separated. I'm away on business a lot, obviously. Lauren has been—difficult at school. She has also managed to dispatch the four nannies I've employed in as many months. Brad intends using all of the above as a way of proving he would be a better guardian for Lauren than I am.'

'But those things don't mean anything.' Casey shook her head. 'Josh has been a little—troubled at school, too. But with his father leaving, the strangeness of having another woman in his father's life, and then their sudden deaths—it's only natural that there should be some sort of reaction. I'm sure that's all that's happening with Lauren, too.'

He shrugged. 'You know that. I know that. Brad obviously sees things differently. He's angry, upset, and he's blaming everything and everyone, including me, for Chloe's death. At the moment he simply doesn't see that he helped form Chloe into the selfish person she undoubtedly was. And no doubt he would make Lauren equally selfish if he were to get his hands on her.'

It wasn't too difficult for Casey to imagine the scenario Xander described.

It *was* difficult, however, to understand how proposing marriage to her was going to solve his dilemma!

'So you think marrying a complete stranger is going to stop him from going ahead with a custody battle?' she said with a frown.

'I think marrying a woman whose young son is already friends with my daughter—she's talked about Josh incessantly the last four months!—and providing Lauren with a stepmother and the stability of a proper family life, is going to stop him from even trying, yes!'

'One big happy family, hmm?' Casey grimaced.

'Can you come up with a better idea?' Xander snapped.

'How about marrying someone you actually love?'

He gave her a pitying glance. 'Don't tell me, after seven years of marriage to a man like Sam Bridges, that you still believe in the love myth? Any more than I do after seven years of marriage to Chloe?'

Her eyes flashed deeply green. 'I think we should leave my marriage out of this.'

'How can we?' Xander asked. 'It's because your marriage was as disastrous as mine that I believed you might be receptive to my proposal—'

'That I might be financially desperate enough to be "receptive" to your proposal you mean, don't you?' Casey bridled angrily, standing up to glare at him. 'I'm sure there must be dozens of women you could find who would marry you without the offer of financial inducement!'

'Someone who would expect more from me than I'm willing to give, you mean?' His mouth twisted cynically. 'I would rather pay up front for the privilege, thank you very much. At least that way we would know exactly where we stood!'

'I don't need your damned charity—'

'No—you're managing just fine on your own, aren't you?" he taunted. 'You're working at two jobs and you still don't have enough money to feed both Josh and yourself. And from the looks of things you've been selling off the furniture a piece at a time, too—'

'Get out, Mr Fraser.' Casey cut him off with quiet determination, her hands clenched into fists at her sides. 'Take your offer and—'

'But you haven't heard what my offer is yet, Casey.'

'I don't need to hear it—'

He ignored her protest. 'As my stepson, Josh would go to the same private schools as Lauren. University later, too. And I would put funds in trust for him to receive when he's twenty-one. Neither he nor you would ever have to worry about money ever again.'

'And in return for all that, what do I give you?' Casey asked, with more than a touch of sarcasm.

'Just your name with mine on a marriage certificate.'

Casey shook her head. 'I understand why you're doing this, Mr Fraser—I really do,' she reiterated as he gave a derisive snort; if anyone tried to take Josh away from her she would do what she had to do to keep him, too. 'But Brad Henderson would never believe in a marriage between the two of us.'

'You're wrong there, Casey,' Xander contradicted her flatly. 'I've had four days to think—to worry about this—and after my seven hellish years of marriage to Chloe, I can assure you I've made my views on marrying again only too plain. Which is why I think a marriage between the two of us—Sam's deserted wife and Chloe's deserted husband—is the only one that Brad would even half believe in.'

'If it was so hellish, why did you stay married to Chloe for so long?' she snapped, stung by how he'd described her as *deserted;* he made her sound like a pair of old shoes Sam had simply laid to one side and forgotten!

'Why did *you* stay married to Bridges?' he retorted.

But Casey knew the answer to the question even before they both answered at the same time.

'Because of Lauren!'

'Because of Josh!'

Xander gave a mocking inclination of his head. 'And then, as it turned out, our fears were all for nothing—because when they did both finally leave neither of them wanted Lauren or Josh! They only wanted each other.'

It was true, Casey acknowledged painfully. Whatever it was that had burnt so fiercely between Sam and Chloe—love, lust, whatever—everything else had been surplus to requirements. Including their two children.

'All I'm asking right now is that you *think* about marrying me, Casey,' Xander encouraged. 'Think of what the two of us marrying could mean to you and Josh, of what I could give you—'

'I said I don't want to hear any of that!' Casey cut in shakily, disturbed by his offer in spite of herself.

Because, the offer of financial security for herself apart, she wanted all those things he had mentioned for Josh, and she hated the fact that she was never going to be able to provide them for him.

And Xander Fraser had to have known that perfectly well when he made his outrageous offer of marriage…

Four days he had said he'd had to think about a solution to his problem, whereas she had only had a matter of minutes to accept that this man really was proposing marriage to her. That the only reason he had chosen her was because he knew she was desperately in need of the financial security he offered.

That he felt confident in making the offer to her because he knew her circumstances were such that he wouldn't need to pretend a love for her he would never feel.

Xander watched the conflicting emotions flickering across Casey's face, realising she was both tempted and repelled by his offer.

He had no idea which emotion was going to win…

CHAPTER FOUR

SHE needed time to think about this, Casey decided. She needed to sit down and think rationally about all that Xander Fraser was offering her.

She no more wanted to marry again than he obviously did—had been just as soured by her unhappy marriage to Sam as he had by his 'hellish' marriage to Chloe.

But that wasn't all that was at stake here, was it? She had Josh's welfare to consider. And, as his stepfather, Xander could give him all the advantages in life that she knew she would never be able to provide for him.

But before making any decision—was she actually *considering* his proposal?—despite his earlier comment, she really needed to know exactly what he would want from her in return.

She looked across at him warily, once again jolted by his sheer physical magnetism. He was an extremely handsome man, his dark good-looks more wild and rugged than the smoothly golden Adonis Sam had been. Yes, Xander was certainly much more vitally physical. That very ruggedness suggested an enjoyment of all the sensual pleasures…

'You said your marriage proposal was a purely business proposition…?' she asked slowly.

He easily returned her gaze, dark brows rising even as a wicked little smile curved his lips. 'Casey, why don't you just come right out and ask whether the marriage would include us sleeping together?'

Colour warmed her cheeks even as she glared at him. 'Well, would it?'

Xander knew he could have continued to play with her. That he would have enjoyed teasing her a little. That he liked the way she blushed when she was embarrassed, resembling a soft, fluffy kitten when it felt itself cornered.

But the situation was too serious for him to prolong this particular conversation. Brad's threats were too painful. He was sure the older man would ultimately lose, but at what cost to Lauren's already delicately balanced emotions?

So instead he shrugged. 'I'll go along with whatever you want.'

'Whatever *I*—?' She broke off incredulously, her eyes wide with shock. 'Are you saying that if I decided I wanted to— wanted to—?'

'To go to bed with me,' Xander inserted helpfully.

She nodded. 'That if I wanted that, you would be willing to— to—?'

'Go to bed with you,' he finished softly. 'Yes, I'd be willing to do that.'

She looked totally stunned now, and Xander realised just how young she was. Perhaps not in years—twenty-seven really wasn't that young—but most definitely in experience, if she didn't know that she could enjoy physical pleasure without being in love with the person she was making love with.

'Why not, Casey?' he added. 'After all, it would be perfectly legal.'

He had a feeling it would be something he would enjoy too. There could be depths to this woman's emotions that she hadn't even discovered fully for herself yet. Yes, he might enjoy administering that TLC he had thought her in need of earlier on…

'It being legal has nothing to do with it!' Casey said indignantly. 'I couldn't just—just go to bed with you because a piece of paper says I can!'

'Why couldn't you?' He came across the room to stand only inches away from her, one of his hands rising to lightly cup the side of her face as his thumb moved caressingly across the fullness of her lower lip. 'You're a very beautiful woman,' he murmured huskily, his gaze roaming over her suddenly pale face. 'Would you find it such a hardship to go to bed with me?' he asked.

Casey found herself mesmerised by those gorgeous firm lips only inches away from her own. What would it be like to feel them moving searchingly against hers? To have him kiss and caress—?

No!

'You would,' Xander said regretfully as she flinched back from him. 'Casey, thousands of people go to bed together every day for no other reason than that piece of paper.'

'Not me!' she assured him firmly, very aware of the way she still trembled from his light caress, and wondering if she was being truthful—to Xander or herself...

She had been in love with Sam when they'd first married. Or at least she had thought she was. It hadn't been long before she had understood that, at only twenty years old, she had probably been too young to realise she was just dazzled by the fact that someone so good-looking and charming as Sam should have fallen in love with her. But by then it had been too late. They had already been married a year, Josh had been a baby only two months old, and her father had recently died.

But she had continued to be married to Sam for a further six years, hadn't she? And it had only been during the last six months of their marriage that the physical side of things had ended completely.

Yes, but that was different, she told herself firmly now. Sam had been her husband—

Only, if she accepted Xander Fraser's marriage proposal he would be her husband, too!

No, she couldn't go through with this! No matter what the financial inducement to make Josh's life more comfortable and her own life free of the continual financial stress...

'I only said it was an option, Casey.' Xander spoke evenly as he saw the sudden panic in her easily readable expression.

Her open emotions were certainly a refreshing change after years of Chloe's deceit and machinations!

Chloe had been the most beautiful woman he had ever set eyes on when he met her seven and a half years ago—a beautiful ebony-haired blue-eyed butterfly who had dazzled and beguiled every man she came into contact with. Including him. And Xander had pursued her relentlessly until he caught her.

But after only a few brief months of marriage he had realised that she truly *was* a butterfly—that her emotions, once given, lasted only fleetingly, before she moved on to the next conquest. And the next. And the next.

Only the fact that Chloe had found herself pregnant at the end of their six-week-long honeymoon—at least Xander had been sure that Lauren was his!—had kept the marriage from ending in divorce once he'd discovered Chloe had taken her first lover.

And that was all their marriage had been—a sham, a front for the dozens of men Chloe had enthralled into her bed. Men she would enjoy, but who couldn't demand too much from her when she had the protection of a powerful husband like Xander Fraser.

He should have divorced her years ago, of course, but the possibility of Chloe taking Lauren with her when she left—the daughter he adored—had prevented him from taking such action.

The fact that he was now being threatened in the same way by Chloe's father was totally unacceptable!

'I would be quite happy with a marriage of convenience, Casey; I'm really not that desperate for a physical relationship with an unwilling wife!' he told her, suddenly harsh after recalling such unwelcome memories.

Where had that anger come from so suddenly? Casey wondered.

And who was to say she would be unwilling…?

Her reaction to his touch just now had told her that she wasn't indifferent to him. And she had already acknowledged to herself earlier that she found this man physically attractive—that he exuded a powerful vitality that would make it impossible ever to ignore him—so how much more disturbing was he going to be if he was her husband? If she was living with him on a permanent basis?

She couldn't be *seriously* thinking of accepting his proposal, could she?

But for Josh's sake, she couldn't *not* seriously think about it!

She had been aware for some weeks that she was fighting a losing battle when it came to paying her bills as well as the mortgage Sam had taken out on this house in order to raise extra capital. She knew she might soon have to give up even trying to hold on to her family home, and find somewhere to rent instead. There would be a few thousand pounds to bank once the house was sold, but nowhere near enough to give Josh all the advantages Xander Fraser was offering if he became her son's stepfather.

So how could she *not* accept Xander's marriage proposal?

She moistened lips that had gone dry. 'If I were to accept—I said *if,* Mr Fraser,' she emphasised, when she saw the look of triumph flare in those dark blue eyes.

'I think you had better call me Xander, don't you?' he invited.

She gave him a scathing glance and deliberately didn't respond to his invitation. A childish gesture, perhaps, but she had a feeling that any advantage she might ever have over Xander Fraser was going to be a small one! 'If I accept, exactly when were you thinking of this marriage taking place?'

Xander damped down his feeling of elation that she was even considering his offer—which was pretty strange for a man who, after Chloe's infidelities, had sworn he would never marry again!

But this was a marriage to be made out of necessity rather than choice, he excused himself. It was for his daughter's sake, not his own—exactly the reason he had settled on Casey Bridges— along with her son Josh, who Lauren adored—in the first place!

He shrugged. 'As soon as we can get a licence, I would have thought. The sooner the better, in fact. Why wait, Casey?' he added persuasively as he once again saw that look of panic in her face. 'The sooner it's done, the matter settled, the sooner we can all get on with our lives.'

He had always liked and respected Brad Henderson, and he knew it was the other man's grief at losing Chloe that was making him behave irrationally at the moment; unfortunately, Xander couldn't afford to give the other man time to come to his senses. He was all too aware of the damage that Brad could wreak in Lauren's life as well as his own before that happened.

The sooner he got Casey Bridges to agree to his marriage proposal the better. He found it distinctly unflattering that she viewed marriage to him in so poor a light—most women he knew would have jumped at the offer.

But then, the women who had been in his life the last year

were as hard and grasping as Chloe had been. He had chosen them deliberately. At least he knew where he stood with women like that. He would certainly never consider—for *any* reason!—offering marriage to one of them.

Casey wasn't like them—would never be like them—which meant he had to back off a little and give her some time to make her decision. Hopefully, she would realise there were far too many advantages for Josh to allow her scruples to stand in the way.

'Why don't you take overnight to think about it, and I'll call you in the morning?' he suggested lightly.

'Overnight?' Casey echoed with another surge of inward panic. Could she take just a few hours to make a decision that would affect the rest of her life?

And Josh's...

Josh. Her weak spot. A weakness Xander Fraser had already exploited to his advantage...

But apparently not her only weakness, Casey acknowledged thoughtfully as she remembered the way she had trembled, the warmth that had coursed through her body, when Xander Fraser had touched her.

Yes, she had to take into account her unmistakable response to all that leashed magnetism, too. She would be foolish not to do so.

She raised her chin and infused her voice with determination. 'Why don't I take my time to think about it and call you when I reach a decision?'

His mouth tightened, his gaze narrowing speculatively as she deliberately turned his suggestion back on him. 'Why don't you?' he finally growled, taking his wallet from the back pocket of his denims to remove a business card and place it on the coffee table. 'But don't take too long, hmm?' he added.

Or what? Casey wondered with a frown as she watched him turn on his heel and leave.

The front door closed behind him seconds later.

Would she find the offer had been rescinded if she dithered too long in giving him an answer?

Would he decide she wasn't worth the trouble and find someone else—someone more receptive—to make his offer of marriage to...?

CHAPTER FIVE

'MR FRASER—'

'*Xander,* Casey,' he insisted as he easily recognised her voice on the other end of the telephone line.

He should; at almost seven o'clock in the evening, he had been waiting all day for this call!

'I've reached a decision,' she told him without preamble.

Xander wasn't in the least reassured by her businesslike tone. He had an uncomfortable feeling that Casey's scruples might have won out, after all.

'Of a sort,' she added, less certainly.

Xander frowned. His patience was already tried to the limit because he'd had to wait all day for her phone call.

It didn't help that Brad's lawyers had already been in touch with his and suggested that they and their client have a meeting in order to 'try and settle custody of Mr Henderson's grand-daughter out of court'!

'Yes?' he prompted, perhaps a shade too tersely.

Casey's mouth felt dry. Her hand was shaking slightly as she held the telephone receiver to her ear, having waited until after she had put Josh to bed before making this call.

She had spent a sleepless night thinking over everything Xander Fraser had said to her, and a distracted day doing exactly the same. And the fact that she knew he wasn't going to like what she had to say certainly wasn't helping her nervousness.

'For God's sake, just say yes or no, Casey!' he bit out as his patience finally snapped.

'I—maybe,' she answered unhelpfully, moistening dry lips. She could feel the tension in Xander's silence on the other end of the line. 'I've thought over everything you said. I can see the benefit to Josh and myself in everything you offered. I just—' She drew in a ragged breath. 'I would need to meet Brad Henderson, to assure myself that his threat is real, before I could possibly give you an answer!' The words came out in a rush as she hurried to get this unpleasantness over with.

It was the only conclusion Casey had come to during the last twenty hours of her thoughts going round and round in circles and always coming back to that one point: maybe Brad Henderson could be made to see how unreasonably he was behaving, that it was grief at his daughter's death that was governing his actions rather than a real belief on his part that Lauren would be better off with him? If the older man could be made to see that then Xander would have no need to think about marrying anyone—least of all Casey.

How was that for shooting herself in the foot?

'Are you serious, Casey?' Xander exclaimed. 'The mood Brad was in the last time we spoke, he would eat you for dinner!'

'Dinner was exactly what I had in mind,' she replied, trying not to feel too concerned. 'In fact, I've already asked for tomorrow evening off work in anticipation of the arrangement. Do you think, if you asked him, he would agree to come? Not here, of course,' she added hastily.

'You're lacking a dining room table, for one thing,' Xander snarled. 'Sorry,' he muttered at her reproving silence, then, 'I can ask him,' he conceded. 'But you had better be prepared for the worst if he agrees,' he warned.

'I think I can cope,' Casey assured him dryly; after dealing with the shock of this man's proposal last night, she was sure she could cope with anything Brad Henderson had to throw at her. 'I think it's the right thing to do—er—Xander.'

'There—that wasn't so hard, now, was it?' he taunted, before adding with a sigh, 'You're pretty insistent on doing what you think is right, aren't you, Casey?'

'I would hate for you to find yourself married to me and then discover you needn't have bothered, after all!' she came back tartly.

He laughed appreciatively, with a husky softness that seemed to move teasingly across Casey's sensitised skin and sent a shiver of awareness down the length of her spine.

'You may not find it so funny if that were to be the case!' she snapped, uncomfortable with the fact that she could be so aware of him just talking to him on the telephone.

This woman was something else, Xander acknowledged wryly. Not only was she hesitating about accepting a marriage proposal from a man who was rich enough to ensure that she never needed to worry about money ever again, but she was also concerned that he should never have cause to regret the marriage!

Incredible.

'I think I would cope, Casey.' He mockingly echoed her earlier assurance to him. 'I'll give Brad a call, and then give you a ring back—okay?' he added briskly, abruptly ending the call. He was not sure what to make of her at all.

It was fine for him to actually *like* the woman he was intending to marry—it would be hell for all of them if he didn't—and it was okay that he found Casey's delicate beauty desirable, too; after all, she might want to change the terms of their marriage some time in the future. But he certainly didn't need to feel anything else for her!

Not even the grudging admiration he now felt after that surprising telephone conversation…

'He hasn't arrived yet, so you can stop looking so apprehensive,' Xander told her the following evening, after the butler had shown Casey into the sitting room.

How could she help but feel anxious when she wasn't even comfortable in Xander's company, let alone in that of his angry ex-father-in-law—who was arriving at any moment?

'You look—wonderful,' Xander said with slow appreciation.

Casey quirked her brows mischievously. 'I don't always look as if I've been dragged through a kitchen backwards!'

'I didn't mean—You're teasing me,' he realised in surprise.

She nodded. 'I thought we had already agreed that I have a sense of humour?' And she was probably going to need it, too!

But at least she knew she *did* look okay. She had spent a lei-surely hour or so in the bathroom before getting ready to come out: blow-drying her hair into silky wisps, keeping her make-up light—a touch of lipstick and blusher, a little mascara empha-sising the length of her lashes. The black knee-length sheath of a dress she wore was several years old, but of good quality nonetheless, and the fact that she knew it suited her slender curves gave an added boost to her confidence.

Hannah—suitably chastened after her behaviour the other evening—had readily agreed to babysit while Casey went out for the evening, and had arrived promptly at seven o'clock, assuring Casey that she had no need to hurry back, that she was quite happy to stay for as long as she wanted to be out.

The daughter of a neighbour three doors down, Hannah was probably bursting with curiosity about this unusual evening out for Casey. But it was a curiosity Casey hadn't felt in the least inclined to satisfy. Time enough, if Casey's marriage to Xander Fraser did go ahead after all, for her neighbours' speculation.

Xander had completely misread her emotion when she'd been shown into the sitting room of his beautiful home—she wasn't feeling apprehensive at all, but slightly in awe of the Fraser home. Electric gates had opened slowly at the end of a long driveway after she had given her name over the intercom, and long rolling lawns had edged that driveway as she drove the half-mile or so to the main house. It was a magnificent house of mellow stone, floodlit from the outside, with lights inside gleaming a welcome from crystal chandeliers.

A magnificent house that *she* might become mistress of…

It also didn't help that, having been shown into this gold and cream sitting room, with its genuine Regency furnishings and a fire burning in the huge Adam fireplace, she felt slightly over-whelmed by how wonderful Xander looked in his black evening suit, with a black bow tie knotted meticulously at the throat of his white silk shirt.

He crossed the room in easy strides to stand just in front of her, his gaze intent as he looked down at her. 'You really do look very beautiful this evening,' he told her huskily.

As a widow with a young son, she was surely too old to blush, Casey told herself, even as she felt the warmth enter her cheeks as Xander repeated his compliment.

'I like the fact that you do this,' Xander murmured, even as his hand moved and his fingers brushed lightly against that blush in her cheeks.

Casey stared up at him, her gaze caught and held by his, her lips slightly parted and her breathing becoming shallow.

The squareness of his jaw looked freshly shaved, his after-shave was alluringly musky, and those sculptured lips curved slightly into a smile as he looked down at her with those dark blue eyes. Eyes that seemed fathomless as Casey suddenly felt herself unable to look away…

'Mr Henderson, sir,' the butler announced haughtily, before what Casey could only describe as a whirlwind swept into the room.

'Xander!' a harsh American voice rasped. 'Who the hell is *this?*' Brad Henderson demanded as he saw Casey standing at Xander's side. 'You didn't tell me we would have company this evening!' he barked at the younger man accusingly.

'That will be all, Hilton.' Xander calmly dismissed the man-servant even as he snaked his hand out to firmly clasp Casey's arm before she would have stepped away from him.

Casey was too stunned at the older man's verbal attack to do anything other than remain in Xander's grasp as she continued to stare across the room at the aggressive American. Whatever she had been expecting—an elderly man bowed down by grief at his daughter's death, perhaps?—it certainly wasn't this tall, loose-limbed, energetically vital man in black evening clothes, his still attractive features defying his sixty-something years.

It was obvious, looking at Brad Henderson, where Chloe had got her looks from. His dark hair was showing signs of grey at the temples, but his blue eyes had the same narrowed shrewdness his daughter's had had.

Even on such brief acquaintance Casey knew Xander was right to fear this man's determination to claim his granddaughter!

It was what she had wanted to know, after all—just not quite so forcefully. Or quite so soon…

Well, she couldn't say Xander hadn't tried to warn her!

'Good evening, Mr Henderson,' she greeted him smoothly, stepping forward to hold her hand out politely.

A hand the older man completely ignored as the hardness of his gaze remained fixed on Xander. 'Who *is* she, Xander?' he demanded scathingly. 'Some woman you've brought in for the evening in the hope of distracting my attention from the real reason I'm here? The *only* reason I'm here,' he added harshly.

Casey's breath caught in her throat at the double insult this man had just thrown out so casually. To imply that Xander would stoop to such behaviour was bad enough, but the slight he'd directed at her was incredibly insulting, considering they hadn't even been introduced to each other.

'I can assure you, Mr Henderson, that—'

'I wasn't talking to you, honey. Well, Xander? Are you going to say anything, or just stand there like a dummy all evening?' he challenged.

Xander could clearly feel Casey's tension as he maintained his grasp on her arm. A perfectly understandable tension, considering Brad was excelling himself with his rudeness this evening.

His father-in-law might believe him capable of many things—most of them Brad had already chosen to volubly share with Xander during their telephone conversation on Sunday evening—but being a procurer of women hadn't so far numbered amongst them!

'Casey…?' Xander prompted, and he looked down at her, raising an eyebrow in enquiry, knowing that the next move was up to her—that he couldn't go any further with this conversation without knowing what her intentions were.

She gave him a startled look, her eyes widening as she understood exactly what he was asking of her.

But she had no choice, Xander acknowledged grimly. Whatever method of introduction he were to use, the mood Brad was in he was sure to misunderstand it. Casey had to be the one who decided what happened next.

She gave him a frown, before glancing across at Brad. Her

back straightened as that glance seemed to bring her to some sort of decision.

Xander found himself holding his breath as he waited to see what that decision was going to be.

Her chin rose challengingly. 'I'm afraid you've completely misunderstood the situation, Mr Henderson,' she told him with quiet dignity. 'Xander did invite you here this evening so that the two of us could meet, yes. But he intended to introduce me to you as his fiancée, and Lauren's future stepmother, rather than anything else you might have assumed!' There was a slight edge to her voice as she finished this pronouncement.

Xander wasn't sure if he wanted to kiss her more at that moment than he had when she had arrived earlier, looking so stunningly, desirably beautiful!

Her announcement had certainly had the desired effect on Brad. He looked momentarily nonplussed, but he recovered quickly, his blue eyes narrowing speculatively as he shot Xander a derisive glance. 'What is this, Xander? A set-up? You're going to keep a so-called fiancée hanging around for a couple of months in the hope of distracting me from a custody suit?'

Xander's hand tightened on Casey's arm as he sensed her bristling indignation. 'Let me introduce the two of you properly,' he drawled. 'Casey—Brad Henderson. Brad, this is Casey Bridges.'

'I don't give a damn—Bridges, did you say?' The older man's attention sharpened noticeably. 'Are you telling me that she's Sam Bridges' widow?'

'One and the same, Brad,' Xander confirmed softly, now able to feel Casey's slight trembling as the older man turned to give her a closer examination.

'You're marrying *Sam Bridges' widow?*' Brad practically shouted incredulously.

'Am I marrying the woman whose husband your daughter seduced from his marriage? The woman who was left alone and penniless after that bastard walked out on her and her son because he found himself a woman who had more money than sense? Yes, I'm marrying Casey, Brad.' He nodded abruptly, his gaze challenging the other man now, knowing that Brad had disliked Sam Bridges almost as much as Xander had.

Brad's face was florid with anger as he glared at the two of them.

'Damn it to hell, Xander! Sam Bridges' widow?' he repeated, shaking his head in utter disbelief.

'That's correct.' Casey was the one to answer huskily. 'I'm sure Xander—and Lauren, of course—would be pleased if you'd care to attend the wedding next month?'

Brad's response to that was completely predictable. 'You haven't heard the last of this, Xander,' he warned fiercely.

But the threat was bluster, pure bluster, and they all knew it...

CHAPTER SIX

'WHEW,' Casey breathed weakly as she collapsed down into one of the sumptuous armchairs. Brad Henderson had stormed out of the room—and the house—only seconds ago. 'What a truly obnoxious man!'

'Here.' Xander sounded amused as he handed her one of the two glasses of brandy he had just poured. 'He really isn't such a bad guy normally,' he excused with a grimace.

Casey looked up at him, brows raised. 'I'll take your word for it!' she said, before taking a reviving sip of the brandy.

It was obviously an expensive brand—unlike the cooking sherry two evenings ago!—and it slid smoothly down her throat to warm her inside and take away some of the shock of the last ten minutes.

'And can I take your announcement to Brad as yours?' Xander asked as he stood beside her chair looking down at her.

Her announcement that she was his fiancée.

That the wedding was going to be next month.

She avoided Xander's searching gaze. 'I'm sure that normally Brad Henderson is a reasonable man.' She wasn't sure of any such thing, considering his behaviour just now, and the selfish way his daughter had turned out, but she was willing to take Xander's word for it if he claimed otherwise. 'But he certainly isn't fit at this moment in time to have the care and control of an already emotionally traumatised six-year-old girl!'

'You didn't answer my question, Casey...' Xander prompted dryly.

No, she hadn't, had she? Because she felt a little shy with him now that the two of them were once again alone—was very aware that before Brad Henderson had interrupted them she had been on the point of raising her face for Xander's kiss.

The man she had just announced she was engaged to marry!

Xander gave a low chuckle. 'I thought he was going to blow a complete gasket when you invited him to attend the wedding next month!'

Casey winced at this reminder that she had done exactly that. And, considering that tomorrow was the start of the next month, the wedding was destined to take place some time in the next four weeks!

'I did, didn't I?' She chewed on her bottom lip as she looked up at Xander. 'Pure bravado on my part, I'm afraid. I don't think I would be too thrilled if he changed his mind and decided to attend after all!'

Xander smiled as he looked down at her, finding this woman more and more intriguing by the minute.

The two earlier occasions they had met, she had been ruffled at having to collect Josh from the house his father had shared with Chloe, let alone seeing Xander there, too.

Two evenings ago she had been tired and looking less than her best after a hard day working at two jobs.

But tonight—tonight she looked a beautiful and sophisticated woman. Someone he had been proud to present to Brad as his future wife.

If, indeed, that was what she was going to be...

His mouth tightened. 'Casey?' he pressed again.

She couldn't prevaricate any more, Casey knew. It was cruel. She had to give him answer. After all, she'd had no qualms about telling Brad Henderson what her decision was to be!

She sat up straighter in the chair. 'After careful consideration, I—I've decided to accept your proposal—your business proposition,' she amended firmly, determined that Xander should realise that as far as she was concerned this was *only* to be a business arrangement.

Not that Casey imagined he thought of it as anything else—

if Chloe Fraser's exotic beauty was anything to go by, she was hardly his type, now, was she?

Which brought her to one of the things that definitely had to be sorted out before any marriage between them took place…

'That's good, Casey.' Xander murmured his satisfaction before she could voice her other concern.

Was it good? she wondered, still filled with doubts about her decision, but knowing—as, no doubt, did Xander!—that it was the only one she could have made.

She couldn't quite meet his triumphant gaze. 'Obviously we still have to work out the—details of the arrangement—'

'Dinner is served, Mr Fraser.' The tall, imposing butler stood in the doorway, looking completely unconcerned by the fact that there were now only two people left to eat the meal that had been intended for three. Although Casey didn't doubt that Hilton, and the rest of the household servants, were all well aware of the way Brad Henderson had stormed out of the house minutes ago. If not the reason for it!

'Shall we…?' Xander held out his arm to take her through to the dining room.

She didn't really need to stay to dinner now that Brad Henderson had left so suddenly, Casey realised. Although it would probably look even more odd to the staff if she were to leave without eating too!

'Of course,' she answered, and she stood up to place her empty brandy glass down on a side table, her hand trembling slightly as she moved to place her hand in the crook of the arm he held out to her.

'Bring some champagne through, would you, Hilton?' Xander instructed the butler.

Champagne?

To toast their engagement, Casey realised.

Or, rather, she corrected herself firmly, to seal their bargain.

The decision made, the commitment voiced, Casey could feel her panic starting to rise again at exactly what she had done.

She didn't doubt that Josh would blossom in the ease and comfort to be found in the Fraser household, nor that her young son would be thrilled at finding Lauren was to be his stepsister, and he would benefit from a change of school, too.

Her anxiety was more because she still wasn't sure quite what *her* role was going to be!

Xander's wife, obviously.

No doubt his hostess, too, if he entertained.

But what else?

'Stop worrying so much,' Xander murmured close to her ear as he pulled out a dining room chair for her to sit down. 'It will all work out—you'll see,' he promised.

Would it? Casey wondered, slightly disconcerted by the warmth of his breath against her neck. Would it really?

The fact that the high-ceilinged, ornately decorated dining room was formally set for two—the third placing having been hastily removed, no doubt—didn't exactly instil her with confidence, either. She couldn't help but notice that the snowy white napkins, cut-glass wine goblets and the silver candelabra with candles already alight were a complete contrast to her own cramped kitchen, where most of their last conversation had taken place.

Once again Xander watched the play of emotions that flittered across Casey's telling face. He looked up to give Hilton a frowning glance as the other man returned carrying a silver tray with the requested bottle of champagne and two glass flutes.

'Just leave it on the side there, Hilton,' he said impatiently. 'I'll deal with it myself,' he added less harshly, shooting the butler an apologetic glance as he did so; after all, it wasn't the other man's fault that Xander's bride-to-be was becoming jittery now that she had actually committed herself to the marriage.

'Very well, sir,' the elderly man acknowledged with an inclination of his silvery head, before quietly leaving.

Xander crossed the room to pick up the chilled bottle wrapped in a white linen napkin and loosen the cork; perhaps if Casey got some champagne inside her she might start to relax again.

The sparkling wine poured, he moved across the room to hand her one of the two-thirds-full glasses before raising his own glass. 'To us,' he toasted huskily.

Casey swallowed hard, her fingers tight around the delicate

champagne flute. 'To us,' she echoed awkwardly, before taking a grateful gulp of the bubbly wine.

Except it didn't quite work out that way. The chilled wine hit the back of her throat, which was tight with nervousness, and then refused to go down!

She began to cough and choke as the bubbly liquid went up her nose, causing her eyes to water, too, holding the glass away from her so that she shouldn't spill the rest of the champagne down herself or over the ornate Aubusson carpet.

She couldn't even see properly when Xander took the glass from her unresisting fingers, patting her lightly on the back as he stood in front of her to use one of the snowy white napkins to wipe away the tears that were now streaming down her face.

This was just too embarrassing, too awful, on top of everything else! What on earth was Xander going to think of her? That she was too gauche even to drink champagne properly without—

Casey became suddenly still as, the choking stopped, her cheeks wiped, she found herself standing only inches away from Xander, looking up into the handsome ruggedness of his face.

Her breath felt strangled in the tightness of her throat and she was completely captured by the sensual heat of Xander's gaze, her heart starting to beat so loudly that she was sure he must be able to hear it, too. She felt so sensitised, so aware, that it seemed as if she could feel the blood rushing through her veins.

She must look a fright, an absolute mess—her eyes teary, her nose red, her cheeks flushed—

None of which seemed to bother Xander in the slightest as he slowly lowered his head and his mouth claimed hers.

Casey melted against him as his arms moved about her waist to pull her into the hardness of his body, and the soft flick of his tongue against her lips encouraged them to part so he could deepen the kiss.

Her own arms moved up, her hands gripping his shoulders to feel the ripple of muscles there, the promise of power as he tensed beneath her touch—a leashed power that she sensed could be so easily released, overwhelming her...

One of his hands caressed the length of her spine as his mouth continued to plunder hers, fingers light against her before his hand cupped the curve of her bottom and drew her even closer against him.

She could feel his body, that leanly muscled force, hard with desire, pulsing against her thighs, filling her with the warmth of her own rising need—a need that was rapidly spiralling out of control—

'Mr James is on the telephone from New York, Mr Fraser,' a voice interrupted them regretfully.

Casey drew back guiltily and turned to look at the butler, standing so stiffly in the open doorway. She couldn't miss seeing the amusement in Xander's gaze before she pulled abruptly away from him to move over to the window and stare out sightlessly into the darkening evening.

What was she *doing*?

Minutes ago she had realised that any relationship between herself and Xander had to be clearly defined—that they would both need to know exactly what each would expect from the other during their marriage—and that it wouldn't include any sort of physical relationship between the two of them.

What had happened between them just now only increased the urgency for that conversation!

'I'll take the call in my study, thanks, Hilton,' Xander said. 'That will be all,' he added, dismissing his servant and waiting for the other man to leave before turning back to Casey. 'We—'

'Please go and take your call, Xander,' she told him shakily, without turning.

Xander stared in frustration at the rigidity of the slender back Casey kept so firmly turned towards him.

Maybe kissing her hadn't been the most sensible thing in the world. But, no matter what she might be thinking now, it hadn't been the worst thing that could have happened, either. The two of them were getting married, for goodness' sake, and if their response to each other just now was anything to go by then it didn't have to be a celibate marriage. For either of them.

'Casey—'

'Would you please go and take your call, Xander?' Her voice was brittle with the tension obvious in her expression as she turned to face him. 'And then I think it would be a good idea for us to discuss the—details of our marriage, when you come back,' she told him coolly.

Details of their marriage?

She had mentioned something about those details earlier, too, hadn't she...?

And, if that determined look in her face was any indication, Xander didn't think he was going to particularly like them!

CHAPTER SEVEN

CASEY had her emotions, and herself, firmly under control by the time Xander returned to the dining room ten minutes later.

It had just been a kiss, she tried to persuade herself. A kiss that shouldn't have happened, and must never be repeated, but nevertheless still just a kiss. And once she and Xander had discussed the terms of their marriage she need never worry—fear?—that it would happen again!

Xander seemed to have put the incident behind him too, as he moved once again to hold a chair for her to sit down at the dining table. 'I think we should start to eat some of this delicious meal my cook has prepared for us, don't you?' he suggested, before taking his own seat opposite hers at the twelve-foot-long table.

It would certainly be easier with Xander seated so far away for her to gather her chaotic thoughts together. To start the discussion that had been interrupted twice already.

But she took a sip of the white wine the butler poured to go with their smoked salmon and waited for the man to leave before attempting to do so. 'I think it might be better if there were some sort of formal contract drawn up between us before we marry,' she told Xander, her long lashes fanning over her cheeks as she looked down at her food, rather than down the table at him.

'A formal contract...?' Xander repeated guardedly.

'Yes.' She chanced a glance at him, and as quickly looked away again as she met the hard glitter of his gaze. 'I think that would be best,' she added nervously. 'So that we both know where we stand and what—what to expect of each other.'

A silence heavy with tension stretched out between them. She really wasn't going to be able to eat any of this lovely food at all if Xander continued to look at her so fiercely, his mouth unsmiling, his jaw clenched.

'A prenuptial agreement, you mean?' he finally bit out.

'Something like that, yes.' Casey nodded, relieved that he was the one who had actually given it that label. For her to have done so would have sounded—well, rather materialistic, perhaps.

But it wasn't just her future she was talking about, was it? She had Josh to consider, too. In fact, if it weren't for her young son she would never have considered Xander's businesslike offer of marriage in the first place.

Besides, she had no idea why he was so obviously displeased by this conversation when the marriage of convenience had been his idea. After all, there had to be guidelines, didn't there? For both of them. Otherwise the whole thing would just be a mess.

And so it began, Xander acknowledged with weary cynicism as he leant his elbow on the table and took a swallow of his wine. He somehow hadn't seen Casey Bridges as mercenary, but he really should have known better. He hadn't met a woman yet who wasn't.

'And what exactly do you have in mind for the contents of this prenuptial agreement?' he asked, almost pinning her to her chair with the force of his piercing gaze.

She made a fluttering movement with her hands. 'I don't know— Well, I would obviously like something in writing concerning the security of Josh's future,' she amended quickly, as Xander raised dark, mocking brows at her prevarication.

He showed his teeth in a humourless smile. 'And of course your own?'

Casey really wished he would stop looking at her like that. Almost as if she were a specimen he had placed under a microscope!

She shook her head. 'I'm more interested in securing Josh's future than my own.'

'Oh, come, Casey—let's not be coy about this,' he drawled, ignoring the food in front of him but continuing to drink his wine. 'Once your house is sold, and you move here, I will obviously pay all household bills, school fees, and so on, but I appreciate you will need access to money of your own for other—expenses,' he rasped. 'In return you will be expected to give up both the jobs you have been working at in order to become a full-time mother to Lauren and Josh.'

Well…yes. She had already worked that out. It wouldn't be too much of a hardship when being a full-time mother was exactly what she had always been—until Sam's desertion a year ago had forced her to juggle motherhood with two jobs in order to support them both. She accepted that it might not be every woman's ideal to be a full-time mother, but she had always enjoyed the role, and had no doubt she would enjoy being stepmother to Lauren, too.

Although she wasn't so sure about selling her family home…

What if Xander changed his mind and this arrangement only lasted a few months? Brad Henderson might calm down more quickly than Xander expected, and so remove the threat of a court battle over Lauren, in which case he wouldn't need a wife any more.

Whereas she would still need a home for Josh and herself…

These were exactly the sort of details that needed to be worked out before they were married, so she had no idea why Xander should continue to look at her in that sceptical way.

'Is that all?' he snapped.

'Er—no. There's also the matter of the—the intimacy, or lack of it, in our relationship,' she added uncomfortably. 'Of course I accept that you're only in your thirties,' she rushed on, before she lost all her courage under Xander's steely gaze, 'that you will want—er—have needs… But as long as your—relationships are kept discreet, I see no reason why they should interfere with our arrangement in the slightest,' she concluded awkwardly.

Xander continued to look at her for several long seconds without speaking, his hooded blue gaze unreadable. 'You don't think,' he finally said softly, 'that after our earlier—exploration of the possibility, perhaps it might be easier—less complicated—if we were to have that sort of relationship ourselves, in order to satisfy those *needs?*'

No, she didn't!

She didn't care about his previous claim that there were thousands of couples who had a sexual relationship but didn't love each other. She had already had that with Sam, and she had no intention of repeating the experience with Xander Fraser!

'No, I don't,' she told him firmly.

Xander's fingers clenched so tightly around his wine glass that he was in danger of breaking it. Damn it, that earlier kiss might have been a little—unwise on his part, and the timing absolutely lousy, but couldn't this woman see that there was a sexual attraction between the two of them that they would be foolish to ignore?

That it could be dangerous to ignore!

Did she seriously expect them to live together in close proximity, as husband and wife, and not explore the possibilities of the desire they obviously felt for each other?

He could see that she did. That green gaze was clear and determined as she looked down the table at him so intently.

'We will, of course, have separate bedrooms,' she added briskly.

That would be no hardship—he and Chloe had occupied separate bedrooms for years, by his choice!

He raised a mocking eyebrow. 'And what of your own— needs? Do you intend to satisfy them *discreetly* too?' His voice hardened. He was not at all happy with the thought.

The blush that he found so intriguing once again brightened her cheeks. 'Certainly not!' she denied indignantly.

Xander frowned, but something inside him eased a little, and he loosened his death-grip on the wine glass before he shattered it. 'Then what do you intend doing about them?'

She shook her head, the candlelight bringing out the gold highlights in her hair. 'I don't intend doing anything about them!' she assured him tartly. 'The—physical side of marriage is not something that interests me in the slightest.'

She really thought she meant that, Xander realised as he took in the set of her mouth and the determined tilt of her chin.

For a woman who had been married for seven years, who had a six-year-old son, Casey was surprisingly naïve if she didn't realise exactly how sexually responsive she was—of how she had melted against him minutes ago, her mouth as hungry as his own.

Xander's gaze narrowed as he wondered again about her marriage to Sam Bridges.

He had despised the other man almost as much as he had despised Chloe—had thought them two of a kind, considering only their own interests of importance. But had that selfishness also permeated Bridges' physical relationship with his own wife?

What business was it of his? Xander instantly rebuked himself; Casey was very firmly setting down the terms of their marriage, making it perfectly clear that the financial security he offered was all that interested her. That he would have to look elsewhere if he wanted to satisfy his physical 'needs'!

'Fine.' He gave a sharp inclination of his head. 'Is there anything else you want written into the contract besides what we've already discussed?'

Casey looked at him uncertainly, knowing she had displeased him in some way, but completely at a loss to understand how. She was being reasonable, wasn't she? More than reasonable, she would have thought.

'No, there's nothing else,' she confirmed.

'Then I'll go ahead and make the necessary arrangements.'

The arrangements for their wedding.

The arrangements for her and Josh to move into this house.

The arrangements for her to be Xander Fraser's wife. In name only…!

CHAPTER EIGHT

For Xander, the three weeks leading up to their wedding day were some of the most puzzling—and frustrating—he had ever known.

Used to making decisions, to controlling his multimillion-pound production company both here and in America, he found dealing with the complexity of the woman who had agreed to become his wife—in name only!—more challenging than anything or anyone else he had ever encountered.

In response to that telephone call from David James he'd initially had to go to New York for five days. While there he had received a telephone call from Brad Henderson, and the older man had made it clear that he didn't believe any marriage between Xander and the widow of Sam Bridges would ever take place.

Which had been enough of a spur—if Xander had needed one!—to set the marriage plans in motion.

Which was when his troubles with Casey had really begun!

Telling the two children of their plans had gone smoothly enough—although Xander had been a little thrown when Josh, with his mother's candour, had innocently asked if he was going to be his new daddy.

Casey had been the one to smooth over that awkwardness by stating that she thought it better if Josh called him Xander for the moment, and Lauren called her Casey.

But following that Casey had flatly refused to comply with his suggestion that she immediately give up her two jobs at the café and the hotel restaurant, claiming that she still had to live and pay the bills until after they were married.

When he had asked why she hadn't put her house on the market yet, he'd been given the same answer.

His question as to whether or not she had any guests she wished to invite to the wedding had also been met with a negative. Well, he didn't, either.

And she had absolutely refused to even consider his suggestion that she make any changes—either to Fraser House, or the running of it—she deemed fit for the comfort of herself and Josh. She had assured him there would be plenty of time for that later, *if* she deemed it necessary.

This had given him some insight into the reasoning behind Casey not doing any of the things he had asked of her—she wasn't sure that he was going through with the wedding, either!

As a way of showing her he was completely serious about the marriage, he'd had his lawyer draw up the contract Casey had asked for—only to have her request that it be sent on to her own lawyer for perusal.

The bundle of fury that arrived at the house that evening, only two days before the wedding, wasn't what he had been expecting!

He was working on some papers in his study when Hilton announced Casey's arrival. The fact that she was here at all was surprising enough, but the angry glitter in her eyes and the flush to her cheeks were even more so as she stormed into his study seconds later and threw the contract down on his desk in front of him.

'I can't sign this!' She scowled.

Xander frowned darkly. 'Why can't you?'

'Because I can't!' she snapped. 'Because it's wrong! Because it's—it's damned insulting!' she finished furiously, her hands bunched into fists at her sides as she confronted him across the wide width of the leather-topped desk.

She really was beautiful when she was angry, Xander thought abstractedly, even as he wondered exactly which part of the contract she found insulting.

Her face was less strained than it had been a couple of weeks ago—those dark circles beneath her eyes having disappeared, and the hollows of her cheeks having filled out a little.

But as for what was wrong with the contract, he had no idea.

He had given her what she'd asked for, hadn't he? Financial security for herself and Josh. So what the hell was the problem?

Casey stood her ground when Xander stood up to move round and rest his hips against the front of the desk. But the movement brought him dangerously close to her in the process, making her totally aware of him—of his warmth, of the air of sensuality that he held in control but which was never far beneath the surface whenever the two of them met.

Not that she showed by the flickering of an eyelid that she was in the least disconcerted by his close proximity. Xander Fraser was a man used to having his own way. She had quickly learnt that this last few weeks. But, as a woman who had become used to running her own life, and Josh's, this last year, she wasn't about to cede any of her independence without a fight.

'Tell me what's wrong and I'll have my lawyer change it,' he promised.

If he had returned her anger, or even if he had spoken to her in that coldly distant tone he sometimes adopted, Casey knew she would have found it easier to maintain her own fury on reading the contract he'd had drawn up.

As it was, she felt a little like a deflated balloon at his reasonable response. 'I— It's just— *That* paragraph is complete nonsense!' She moved to jab a finger at the offending paragraph in the contract.

She was now even closer to Xander, her arm brushing against his before she moved back abruptly to look at him from beneath lowered lashes.

There was a dark shadow to the squareness of his jaw where he was in need of a shave, and his overlong hair was slightly dishevelled where he'd been running his fingers through it as he'd worked at his desk. Dark hair, that shone with ebony lights… The sort of hair that made Casey long to reach out and touch it, to run her own fingers through its silky length as Xander's mouth once again plundered hers—

Casey gave an inward groan. She'd had a lot of fantasies like this these last couple of weeks—moments when she had found herself thinking of Xander, of the way he had kissed her, caressed her…

Imagining what would have happened if Hilton hadn't interrupted them that evening...

After all her talk of a marriage of convenience between them, her insistence that she wouldn't object to him having other relationships as long as he was discreet, Casey now knew that she found the very idea of Xander being intimately involved with another woman completely abhorrent.

Which was pretty ridiculous when she had absolutely refused to even contemplate the two of *them* having an intimate relationship.

But there was a good reason for that.

A very good reason.

She didn't want Xander to know—for him to discover, just how inept she was at lovemaking. 'Frigid' was one of the words that Sam had used, along with 'unresponsive' and 'cold'.

Sam had not been amused by her inexperience on their wedding night—had been slightly put out that he'd had to be the one to initiate her into lovemaking—and the whole thing had been painful and awkward for Casey. The fact that she had found herself pregnant only three months later had been something of a relief because Sam had claimed to find the whole idea of making love to a pregnant woman repugnant.

Their lovemaking had resumed after Josh's birth, of course, but it had never been something that Casey had enjoyed—more something to be endured.

But she had been attracted to Sam before their marriage—had thought herself in love with him—and look how disastrously that had turned out!

No—no matter how attractive she found Xander, she did not want to repeat the experience with him, to see the same impatience in his face when he found out what a disappointment she was in bed.

Luckily he wasn't looking at her, but at the contract he had picked up, a slight frown between those deep blue eyes as he finally looked up to shake his head. 'I can't see what the problem is—'

'There!' Casey moved forward to point to the appropriate paragraph, drawing in a sharp breath as once again she found herself standing so close to him she could smell the musky tang of his cologne, could see the dark hair that grew lightly on his bared arms beneath the black tee shirt he wore, see the quiet strength of his hands, his fingers long, the nails kept short.

Hands that last night she had actually dreamt of—touching her, caressing her—

'I still don't see it,' Xander protested. 'All it says is "the amount of one million pounds is to be paid into the bank account of Casey Bridges, then to be Casey Fraser, on the day of the marriage"—'

'*All it says?*' Casey repeated incredulously, stepping back slightly. 'A *million pounds,* Xander?'

Xander found himself very aware of the woman standing so close to him. In fact, he acknowledged with self-derision, he had often found himself thinking of Casey lately, when he should have been concentrating on other things.

Apart from Lauren, who was something else entirely, work had always come first with him these last seven years—had been the constant that kept his life with Chloe bearable.

But this past few weeks he had found himself musing about Casey even in the middle of business deals. Found himself wondering about the soft curves of her body, of how it would feel to have her nakedness against him, under him, on top of him. Imagining parting the litheness of her thighs, touching her there, feeling her flower and blossom...

He wanted to touch her, to kiss her, taste her, to watch her face as he slowly, oh, so slowly entered her, and the heat of her engulfed him—

He was doing it again!

Except that this time Casey was standing right here beside him, looking up at him with those huge green eyes, her cheeks flushed, her lips slightly parted, as if waiting for his kiss.

He couldn't fight this any longer, Xander decided achingly, and he reached out to grasp the tops of her arms and pull her hard against him, shutting off her angry words as his mouth captured hers.

He slowly lay back on the desk behind him and took Casey with him, her thighs lying between his parted ones, the softness of her breasts crushed against his chest, as his mouth claimed hers with the fierceness of three weeks' longing.

CHAPTER NINE

CASEY had no idea how she came to be lying on top of Xander on his desktop as his mouth plundered hers—none of the fantasies she'd had about him had ever been *this* immediate—she only knew that she felt empowered, above him like this, as she raised her head slightly to nibble and suck his bottom lip, to taste him as he was tasting her.

Xander groaned low in his throat, his hands moving restlessly along the length of her spine as he encouraged her to deepen the kiss. A move Casey denied him as she took her time running the warmth of her tongue against his parted lips.

But it was her turn to groan with pleasure as she felt Xander push her tee shirt up over her back, his hands, those big warm hands, against the bareness of her flesh, spreading fire wherever they touched.

Casey's hands tangled in the dark thickness of his hair as she kissed him hungrily, her lips apart as he returned that hunger, his tongue plunging into her hotly as she squirmed her hips against his hardened thighs.

Xander broke the kiss to push her tee shirt completely out of his way before his hands moved about her slender waist and he easily lifted her slightly above him, so that his tongue circled and licked the hardened nub of her bared breast.

Casey arched her back as her breasts tingled and swelled to the caress, gasping breathlessly as Xander drew the tightened nipple into the heat of his mouth, sucking and licking, that tingle spreading to her thighs as she moved rhythmically against him.

He was so hard against her, his hardness rubbing against the heated centre of her even as his mouth continued its attention on her breast.

She was on fire, her eyes closed, her breathing ragged, the heat between her thighs becoming unbearable as Xander's hand cupped and captured her other breast, his thumb moving caressingly against the hard tip in the same rhythm as he sucked its twin.

'Xander, I can't—!'

'Yes, you can,' he assured her gruffly as he released her to roll over, so that she was the one now lying on the desktop, his gaze held hers as his hand moved to unsnap the button on her denims, before reaching beneath to unerringly seek the centre of her need.

As soon as he touched her there Casey arched against him, wanting more, wanting something—

Xander's mouth claimed hers even as he found her centre, his thumb moving softly against the swollen nub even as his fingers touched her moisture, circling but not yet entering.

Casey breathed shallowly, her eyes closed as she gave herself up to the pleasure she could feel deep inside her—a pleasure that spread and warmed, burned as Xander increased the rhythm of his caress, as his fingers finally entered her to move in the same rhythm.

She couldn't take any more—felt as if she were about to explode with pleasure—needed, needed—

She gasped, her eyes wide, as Xander satisfied that need with the firm caress of his thumb. Casey exploded around him in spasms of unrelenting pleasure as she stared up at him in the sheer wonder of her release, the whole of her body throbbing with the ecstasy he'd made her feel.

Xander watched her unashamedly as she found her release, his caresses continuing until he was sure she was completely spent, until he had given her every last moment of pleasure.

Then he bent his head to once again claim her lips with his, his caresses soothing now, gentling, as he smoothed her tee shirt back over her breasts before entangling his hands in the silkiness of her hair, his lips moving to kiss the tiny shell of her ear before trailing down the column of her throat to the tiny pulse throbbing at its base.

Casey moved restlessly beside him. 'But you didn't—' She drew in a shaky breath. 'You haven't—'

He raised his head to look down into her stricken face. Her cheeks were flushed, her eyes darkened by dilated pupils, and she couldn't quite meet his gaze. 'I don't need to,' he assured her gruffly.

And he didn't. What had happened just now, seeing and feeling Casey's pleasure, had been the most erotic experience he had ever had in his life. The throbbing of his own body was sweet evidence of that.

Casey's skin was like velvet, her breasts so small and perfect, so responsive to his hands, lips and tongue. *All* of her was so responsive that he felt that to take his own pleasure would ruin something that was already perfect.

'I don't need to,' he repeated huskily, smiling down at her as his hand moved to lightly caress one pink cheek.

Casey stared up at him wordlessly. Why didn't he need to? Sam had always—

Now wasn't the time to think about Sam, or their marriage! Xander had just—

No, *she* had just climaxed—for the first time in her life.

Ever.

And it had been the most wonderful experience she had ever known. She had never dreamt—never realised—

What must Xander think of her?

She had come here to tell him that one of the details in the contract he'd had drawn up outlining the terms of their marriage was unacceptable to her, and had ended up having an orgasm on his desktop!

Not only that, but Xander had obviously found her lack of control so shocking that it had killed his own desire!

She turned her head away. 'Would you let me up, please?' She spoke quietly.

'Casey—'

'Just let me up, Xander!' Her voice rose forcefully as she turned to glare at him.

Sighing, he complied, standing up to look away as she moved to adjust the fastening of her denims.

Casey swayed dizzily as she stood up, her legs feeling weak from the onslaught that had just racked her body, still aware of that tingling sensation between her thighs.

She closed her eyes briefly, wondering how she was ever going to be in Xander's company again without remembering—remembering how she had—

'I have to get to work,' she told him abruptly.

Xander turned slowly to look at her, frowning as he saw the closed expression on her face—her eyes unreadable, her mouth set hard with determination. 'Don't you think we need to sit down and talk more than you need to go to work?' he finally suggested.

'Talk about what?' she challenged.

Yes—talk about what? Xander wondered as he continued to look at her.

The last half an hour might have been the most incredibly erotic experience of his life, but it obviously hadn't meant the same to Casey...

He drew in a deep breath before moving quickly away from her. He was afraid of what he might do if he didn't!

'So I'm supposed to ignore what just happened, huh?' he growled.

She blinked, swallowing hard before answering. 'I think that might be for the best, don't you?'

It wasn't a question, and Xander didn't bother granting it an answer. If she could forget what had just happened then he would obviously be wasting his time talking about it.

'Just put in whatever you want that paragraph to say.' He held out a pen and the contract without looking at her, his clenched hands returning to his sides as he resisted the impulse to reach out and kiss her senseless as she made the necessary adjustment.

Despite the sexual attraction that existed between them, Casey obviously regretted having given in to that attraction. She was making it perfectly clear that she didn't want a repeat of it, either, that it had meant nothing to her.

All this marriage meant to Casey—all it would *ever* mean to her—was financial security. And the sooner he got used to that idea the better.

'Fine.' He nodded as she placed the adjusted contract back down on the desk. 'As Josh and Lauren won't be at the wedding on Friday, I think it would be a good idea, after you and Josh have moved in here tomorrow afternoon, for the two children to stay up and have dinner with us. I know it's a school day the following morning,' he continued as she would have spoken, 'but they need to feel a part of this.'

Oh, God. She and Josh moved in here tomorrow afternoon…!

How could she go through with this after what had just happened?

But how could she not? She had already handed in her notice at her two jobs—had already finished at the café earlier today. This was the last evening she would be working at the hotel. Her own and Josh's things were packed back at the house, ready to move in here tomorrow.

In less than forty-eight hours she was due to become wife to Xander.

A man she had just discovered could so easily take her to the heights of pleasure.

A man she had come to like these last three weeks.

A man she had come to…love?

She gave him a startled look. *Did* she love Xander? Had she fallen in love with the man who was only marrying her to provide a mother for his daughter, to stop his father-in-law from attempting a custody suit for that daughter?

Could she really have been so stupid?

'What is it now?' Xander asked wearily as he watched the play of emotions cross Casey's face. 'After what just happened, you want it actually written into the contract that we maintain separate bedrooms? Fine.' He nodded. 'You want it in writing that there won't be a repeat of just now? Again, fine,' he snarled. 'Now, if you wouldn't mind, Casey, I have some work to do, too.' He moved pointedly to sit back behind his desk, too tired, too bone-weary now, to engage in any more verbal battles with this woman this evening.

Casey's face had first flushed, and then paled at his outburst. 'That won't be necessary,' she told him coldly. 'Just the adjustment I've made will be quite sufficient.'

'Then don't let me keep you. I would *so* hate for you to be late to work,' he added. And he knew he sounded so like Lauren when she was in a fit of childish pique that he was surprised Casey didn't tell him to grow up.

She didn't—simply giving him one last pained look before turning on her heel and making a dignified exit, her head held high.

What an idiot he'd been, Xander instantly berated himself.

Had he really thought, when Casey had come here to complain that a million-pound settlement on her wasn't enough, that the two of them making love would make any difference to her completely financial motivation for marrying him?

He was a fool.

Not only that, but he had been so beguiled, so enchanted with Casey's loss of control, that he hadn't even wanted to find his own release in the warmth of her body—had found her pleasure more than enough to satisfy him.

He was worse than a fool.

Chloe had used her body to manipulate and control him too. Until he had become wise to her machinations and refused even to share her bed any more.

He couldn't believe he had fallen for that trick a second time!

How much more than a million did Casey want? How much did she think that sexual encounter was worth?

Xander's eyes glittered angrily as he picked up the contract. But his anger quickly turned to a puzzled frown when he looked down at the adjustment Casey had made.

That whole paragraph concerning the settlement of money directly on Casey on the day of their marriage had been completely erased, with firm, black strokes of his pen!

Casey didn't personally want *any* settlement of money from him.

He didn't feel angry or puzzled any more—he felt stunned!

CHAPTER TEN

'It's going to be great living here, isn't it, Mummy?' Josh said excitedly as the two of them returned to his new bedroom, after sharing a swim with Lauren in the indoor pool at the back of Fraser House.

Oh, yes—great, Casey echoed wearily in her head, outwardly giving her blond-haired young son an encouraging smile as she went through to the adjoining bathroom to run the shower for him.

The two of them had moved in that afternoon, as planned. Xander had been conspicuously absent when they did so—for which Casey had been very grateful, still not sure how she was going to face him again after yesterday evening.

The worst part about it, as far as Casey was concerned, was that she only had to close her eyes to relive the way Xander had kissed and caressed her, her body tingling anew as she remembered how it had felt when she had completely lost control.

Wonderful.

Like nothing else she had ever known in her life.

Something she craved—longed to have happen again!

But she knew that she couldn't let it.

There was absolutely no point in continuing to explore a sexual relationship with Xander. Especially when his comments afterwards, concerning the inclusion of clauses in their contract about separate bedrooms and there being no repeat of what had happened between them, had to mean that their time together couldn't have meant the same to him as it had to her. It was obviously no hardship on his part to forego an intimate relationship with her.

How could it be? Xander was gorgeous, extremely sexy, and there had to have been dozens of woman in his life—both before and since his marriage to Chloe. Unlike Casey, who had previously only ever known Sam as a lover. And even that one time with Xander had shown her just how awful Sam's lovemaking had been in comparison!

Once Sam had realised on their wedding night that she was still a virgin, he had never particularly cared about initiating her into pleasure.

He'd seemed to think she should know what to do—that her inexperience was nothing but a liability he had no time for, and it was her own fault she never reached a climax in their lovemaking.

And she had accepted what he told her—had been sure that he was right, that there must be something wrong with her because she didn't enjoy sex with her own husband.

She had enjoyed it with Xander last night.

Because she had instinctively known what to do with Xander!

He had allowed her to kiss and caress him, pulling her on top of him as he'd invited her to take the initiative.

And he had felt so good. So—

'Is everything okay?'

She spun round guiltily as Xander suddenly spoke behind her, spraying him with water because she still held the showerhead in her hand.

'Thanks!' he murmured ruefully as he looked down at the water soaking into his pristine white shirt.

'Oh, Lord!' Casey gasped her dismay as she realised what she had done, quickly turning off the water to drop the shower head into the bath.

She picked up a towel and moved across the room to wipe ineffectually at his shirt-front, her movements slowing and then finally stopping when she found her gaze caught and held by the way the shirt clung to him, the material almost see-through now, the dark hair on his chest clearly visible.

She looked up at him from beneath lowered lashes, and then

quickly looked away again as she found him looking down at her
with enigmatic blue eyes.

'I'm really sorry about that,' she mumbled awkwardly.

'Forget it,' he dismissed.

Forget the way the shirt was clinging to him, outlining his
muscled arms, the powerful expanse of his chest, making him
look more sexy than if he actually hadn't been wearing a shirt at
all? Impossible!

'Perhaps you had better go and change—'

'I said forget it, Casey. I'm more interested in whether or not
you have everything you need,' he said gently.

She swallowed hard, knowing that he wouldn't want to hear
what she needed at that moment!

Because she needed *him*. His arms about her. His mouth on
hers. His hands caressing her.

She moistened lips that had gone suddenly dry. 'Josh and I
are fine. Thank you,' she added.

'I've already spoken to Josh and established that he's more than
happy. Lauren, too,' Xander said. 'I was asking about *you*, Casey.'

What did he want her to say? That she was fine, too? That all
of this was fine with her? That she was already as comfortable
with her drastic change in lifestyle as Josh obviously was? That
she wasn't bothered by the fact that Xander's idea of separate
bedrooms was actually to have adjoining ones?

What she really wanted to say was that she had made a mistake
in even *thinking* that she could go through with a marriage of convenience now that she had realised how she felt about him.

That in the three short weeks she had known him she had
fallen in love with him...

Oh, yes—she could just see herself telling Xander all of that!

'Everything is fine.' She nodded, still not able to meet his gaze.

How could she, when yesterday evening she had behaved
like a complete wanton in his arms and for every hour since then
had wanted a repeat of what they'd done?

Xander's gaze rested thoughtfully on her bent head as he saw
her total unease in his company—not that it was surprising after
what had happened last night.

Casey had made it perfectly clear to him—several times!—that she wasn't interested in a physical relationship with him.

Something he'd had no trouble in totally ignoring once he had her in his arms.

In fact, a part of him had been surprised to discover she had moved in as planned when he'd got home this evening. He had half expected that she might have decided she couldn't go through with marrying him, after all.

What the hell had he been thinking of when he'd taken her on his desktop like that?

The problem was he hadn't been thinking at all—had been driven to kiss and caress every silken inch of her, to feel her nakedness against him, to taste her.

Not what she would have been expecting when she'd only come to discuss some changes to the contract he'd had drawn up!

Changes he had spent most of the day trying to make sense of—when he hadn't been thinking of how Casey tasted and felt, that was!

This woman—a woman he had three weeks ago cold-bloodedly decided to marry—made him feel anything but cold-blooded. Even standing next to her now, his wet shirt clinging to him uncomfortably, he knew that he wanted her. Wanted her wild and wanton beneath him as he entered her, as he felt himself engulfed by her, possessed by her, as they both reached a shuddering climax this time.

It had all seemed so simple when he'd first come up with this plan—so uncomplicated: marriage to a woman he didn't love, who made no pretence of loving him, and both of them knowing exactly what was expected, wanted from the marriage.

After last night it didn't seem that uncomplicated at all.

There was no way—absolutely no way—he was going to be able to share this house with her, occupy the adjoining bedroom to hers, without wanting to make love to her again.

In fact, as things stood, he wasn't sure that *he* could go through with this marriage of convenience at all!

'I need to talk to you, Casey,' he rasped. 'Alone,' he added, as Josh could be heard singing happily in the adjoining bedroom.

She gave him a startled look. 'I—we're due to have dinner with the children,' she reminded him.

He nodded curtly, well aware that he was the one to have suggested the arrangement. He just hadn't realised at the time how desperately he would need to be alone with Casey.

'Once they're both in bed will do,' he said.

'I—of course,' Casey agreed slowly, shooting him an uncertain glance as she did so.

Xander's eyes, as he returned her gaze, were dark and unreadable—although the harsh expression on his face certainly wasn't encouraging.

What did he need to speak to her about so urgently? she wondered, with a sickening jolt in her stomach.

Had he spoken to Brad Henderson today and worked out some sort of compromise with him?

Had Xander decided not to go ahead with their marriage, after all?

CHAPTER ELEVEN

SITTING through dinner, with Xander now looking incredibly sexy in black trousers and a black silk shirt that showed off the broad width of his shoulders and the flatness of his stomach, trying to pretend, for Josh and Lauren's sake, that they really were going to be one big, happy family, was absolutely excruciating for Casey.

Especially when, as the minutes slowly passed, and the brooding Xander seemed to have trouble addressing even the most casual of remarks to her, it became more and more obvious he wished her anywhere but here in his home.

If he had changed his mind—if he had decided not to go ahead with the marriage—then he should have sought her out earlier today and told her so. Before she'd had a chance to actually move herself and Josh in here, Casey thought. It was going to be much harder for all of them if she and Josh simply had to move out again.

When Lauren requested that Casey be the one to put her to bed as well as Josh, Casey felt even more of a fraud, and her cheeks were flushed with anger when she returned to the sitting room minutes later, to find Xander standing beside the fireplace enjoying a glass of brandy.

'Like one?' He held up the bulbous glass.

'Am I going to need one?' she returned sharply.

'That depends on your perspective on things!'

Casey's mouth set unhappily. 'In that case, I'll have some,' she said, before moving to stand on the other side of the fireplace to stare down sightlessly at the crackling flames as she waited for Xander to return with the brandy.

She was wearing a green off-the-shoulder dress this evening, Xander noted admiringly, glancing across at her as he poured her brandy and refreshed his own glass. The soft material clung to the pert thrust of her breasts and the slender lines of her waist and thighs.

In fact, Xander had been looking at her admiringly all evening. Casey was beautiful—more subtly, quietly so than Chloe had ever been, but it was a beauty that came from within. He didn't doubt that in fifty years or so Casey would still be radiantly lovely.

Fifty years or so…

Where would *he* be in fifty years?

Still here at Fraser House, he suspected, with Lauren and Josh having left long ago to make their own way in the world. Casey would be gone too, once there were no children to bind them together. So it would be just Xander, rattling around in a house that would no longer have a family in it to make it a home.

The thought of growing old alone had never bothered him. His marriage to Chloe had been over for years before she'd actually left, and he had long been used to being alone.

Alone was good. Alone was undemanding. Alone was the freedom to do what he wanted, when he wanted. Alone was uncomplicated.

Alone sucked!

He crossed the room to hand Casey her glass of brandy, a frown creasing his brow as he noted the way she deliberately avoided her hand coming into contact with his.

She could no longer even bear for him to touch her casually!

He took a swallow of his own brandy before speaking. 'Casey—'

'I'm sorry to interrupt, Mr Fraser—'

'Not now, Hilton!' Xander growled, and he turned to glare at the manservant standing in the doorway.

Damn it, he had never realised what an intrusion household staff could be until Casey came into his life! Every time he tried to talk to her, it seemed for one reason or another Hilton came in and interrupted.

Except yesterday evening, in Xander's study…

It was probably just as well that the butler hadn't walked in on that particular scene!

The elderly man had the grace to look apologetic. 'I really am sorry for the interruption, Mr Fraser, but Mr Henderson has called—'

'Tell him I'll ring him back later,' Xander instructed, not at all interested in yet another confrontation with his ex-father-in-law.

'You misunderstand me, Mr Fraser,' Hilton persisted. 'When I said he had called, I meant that he's here—at the house.'

'Here?' Xander repeated, with a scowl. 'Now?'

'He's waiting in the hallway, sir.'

Xander looked at Casey, noting that her eyes were wide with an apprehension she couldn't hide. 'If you would rather go upstairs while I talk to Brad…?'

He was offering her a way out, Casey realised. A chance to escape any further insults from his ex-father-in-law.

She straightened her shoulders, her chin rising. 'No, I don't think so, thank you,' she refused quietly, surprised when Xander reached out and gave her hand a reassuring squeeze.

'Good girl,' he murmured approvingly, before turning back to the waiting butler. 'Show Mr Henderson in, Hilton.'

Casey was aware of Xander's hand still holding hers when Brad Henderson was shown into the room. The older man's gaze narrowed immediately as he took in that outward show of intimacy.

Which was probably why Xander had done it, Casey thought.

Obviously the two men hadn't come to any compromise after all—so what had Xander needed to talk to her about so urgently earlier on?

'Brad,' Xander greeted him curtly, once the three of them were alone.

'Xander,' the older man acknowledged with a nod. 'Mrs Bridges,' he added, surprisingly.

'Casey will do,' Xander was the one to suggest.

Brad Henderson gave a brief smile. 'I—I believe the two of you are to be married tomorrow?' he began awkwardly.

'Yes, we are,' Xander replied firmly.

Yes, they *were*? Casey thought, relieved.

Xander hadn't changed his mind about the marriage, after all?

Or was he just saying the wedding was going ahead for the other man's benefit…?

'Yes. Well.' Brad Henderson looked decidedly uncomfortable. 'I—' He broke off, breathing heavily.

'Can I get you a drink, Brad?' Xander offered gently. 'You look as if you could do with one.'

The older man quirked a rueful brow. 'That obvious, is it?'

'Yes,' Xander drawled, releasing Casey's hand to move across the room to the drinks cabinet. 'Bourbon on the rocks?'

'Thanks,' the other man accepted, glancing at Casey once Xander had handed him his drink. 'I believe I owe you an apology, Mrs—Casey,' he amended stiffly.

'You do,' Xander agreed, before Casey could think of an appropriate reply. 'You were extremely rude to her three weeks ago,' he pointed out as he moved back to stand at Casey's side.

One thing was becoming very clear to Casey—Brad Henderson had had some sort of change of heart. Perhaps it meant the wedding didn't even need to take place.

It was what she had feared from the beginning, of course. The reason she had insisted on meeting Brad Henderson three weeks ago—to ascertain that his threat was genuine.

Although the reasons for her misgivings now were no longer the same as they had been then!

She had fallen in love with Xander over the last three weeks. She *wanted* to marry him.

She wanted to wake up beside Xander every day for the rest of her life. Wanted to have more children with him. Wanted the two of them to watch all their children grow up together. Wanted to grow old with him…!

Brad tried to smile. 'I'm afraid I wasn't quite myself when we last met, Mrs—Casey,' he offered.

She inclined her head graciously. 'It was perfectly understandable, following your recent loss.'

'Perhaps,' he accepted.

'It wasn't understandable at all after what Casey had already been through,' Xander refuted. 'You were bloody insulting, Brad,' he added grimly. 'To both Casey and myself.'

The other man had put him in an unacceptable position

because of his threats concerning Lauren, and Xander, for one, didn't intend letting him get away with it that easily.

Brad ran a hand through the thickness of his hair and he looked shame-faced. 'I was, wasn't I?' he acknowledged with a grimace. 'I really do apologise, Casey,' he turned to tell her gruffly. 'I—if you and Xander have managed to find some happiness together out of this mess, then I sincerely wish you well.' Brad raised his glass and took a huge swallow of his bourbon. 'I may have been an over-indulgent father, Xander, but I wasn't blind. I always knew that you and Chloe weren't particularly happy together—'

'We weren't happy together at all,' Xander said bluntly, welcoming Brad's apology.

'No. Well.' Brad gave a shuddering sigh. 'I knew that, of course. But she was my daughter, Xander,' he appealed. 'And despite everything I loved her.'

'Of course you did.' Casey was the one to answer him soothingly.

'But that's no excuse, is it, Xander?' Brad looked across at him regretfully. 'I put you in a terrible position three weeks ago, with my threats concerning Lauren.' He gave a self-disgusted shake of his head. 'If it's any consolation, I've come here this evening to eat humble pie.'

Xander watched as Casey moved gracefully across the room to Brad's side, to place her hand lightly on his arm. 'Why don't you sit down for a while, and perhaps the three of us can talk quietly together?' she invited.

She really was the most incredible woman, Xander acknowledged with growing wonder. Most women in the same position, having previously been insulted and ridiculed, would have told Brad just what they thought of him. Chloe certainly would have done. But Casey, being Casey, was being gentle and understanding.

He could only hope for that same gentleness from her when the two of them talked together, once Brad had left.

Brad was just as amazed. 'I can't believe someone like you was ever married to that complete—' He broke off, realising he was about to be rude again. 'Insulting the man isn't going to bring Chloe back,' he acknowledged shakily.

Xander felt for him, he really did, and his own anger faded. He knew what it must be costing the other man to come here this evening and abase himself like this.

Brad continued. 'I want you both to know that I'd no idea Bridges was even married until I called to see Chloe one weekend and Bridges' son Josh was actually staying there with them. Chloe didn't tell me that the two of them setting up home together had broken up two families, not just one. And even once I knew about Josh, Chloe assured me that the marriage had been over long before she'd entered Bridges' life. But that wasn't true either, was it?' He sighed.

Casey felt so sorry for this man. She knew that he must have faced some harsh realities about his daughter in the three weeks since he had met her, and Xander had told him the truth about the break-up of her marriage.

'No, it wasn't.' Xander was the one to answer the other man harshly. 'I told you three weeks ago what really happened.'

'Yes.' Brad Henderson nodded. 'But even then I couldn't believe it—couldn't accept that Chloe had done such a thing. It was only after I spoke to you on the telephone in New York, when you insisted you were telling me the truth, that I sat down and realised how wrong I've been. You've never lied to me in the way that Chloe did, Xander. I want you to know I'm not going ahead with any custody battle over Lauren. I—she's better off with you. And Casey,' he added, with a brief smile in her direction. 'I had better go now.' He stood up abruptly to drain the last of his bourbon, before placing the empty glass on the coffee table. 'I hope that some time in the future you will be able to forgive me for the trouble I've caused, and that—that you will let me see my granddaughter from time to time.' He gave Xander a hopeful look.

Casey looked at Xander, too, willing him not to remain angry with the older man.

At the same time she recognised that Brad Henderson backing down on the custody battle now meant that Xander *definitely* didn't need to marry her!

CHAPTER TWELVE

'WELL...that was pretty traumatic, wasn't it?' she said over-brightly, once Xander had returned from walking Brad out to the door.

Xander looked at her from between narrowed lids, pleased that Brad had backed off from a custody battle over Lauren, and more than happy to forgive the man and assure him that of course he could see his granddaughter—any time he wanted to.

It was the fact that there was now no reason for Casey to marry him that was causing him to frown.

Causing him to frown? He wanted to hit something!

'Another brandy?' he offered.

'I think I've already had enough, thanks,' Casey declined. 'Well, what do we do now?' she asked, in that bright voice that grated Xander's already frayed nerves.

'What do you want to do?' he asked cautiously.

'I don't think that's up to me, do you?'

'Who else is it up to, then?' Xander challenged.

Casey smiled wryly. 'I suppose we should cancel the wedding. Move my own and Josh's things back to the house. You see—it was just as well that I didn't put it on the market.'

She could look a little less happy about this, Xander fumed, wanting to wipe that smile right off her face.

Her heart was definitely breaking, Casey decided, as Xander took his time in answering her. Probably trying to find the words that would cause the least awkwardness, she acknowledged leadenly.

There was nothing he could say that wasn't going to hurt her!

He no longer had any need to marry her. She wasn't going to have more children with him that they could watch grow up together. She most certainly wasn't going to grow old with him!

'It's a little late for Josh and I to move out this evening, so if it's okay with you I think we'll leave it until the morning,' she suggested, trying desperately to keep her voice steady.

'No, that most certainly isn't okay with me!' Xander snarled.

'You want me to wake Josh up and take him away from here *tonight?*' Casey gasped, and she stared across at him incredulously.

Surely he couldn't be that cruel? It was going to be difficult enough explaining to Josh why there was no longer going to be a wedding, or a stepsister and stepfather, without waking him up to tell him that in what was the middle of the night to him!

'No, of *course* I don't want that,' Xander almost roared.

She gave a dazed shake of her head. 'I don't understand…'

Xander's mouth tightened. 'We had—have a deal, Casey. We get married, and I provide for Josh's future, remember?'

Well, of course she remembered. But with Brad Henderson's visit, his apology, surely the reason for their marriage had now been removed…

'Don't worry, Xander, I'm not going to hold you to any of that.' She shrugged. 'After all, neither of us have signed the contract, so there was never actually anything in writing, was there? Besides, the fact that the marriage isn't going to take place makes that contract null and void anyway.'

Xander's expression was stormy. His hands clenched at his sides in an effort to control his rising temper.

Casey was being so damned calm about all of this. So understanding. So unconcerned!

He drew in a ragged breath. 'You don't think we should consider going ahead with the marriage, anyway?' he finally managed to bite out through gritted teeth.

Her eyes widened. 'Why on earth would we do that?'

Because the thought of her just walking out of his life tomorrow was totally unacceptable! Because he wanted to marry her!

But not on the terms they had agreed. Oh, no, he wanted more than that. Much more than that…

'It seemed like a good idea yesterday, so why not today?' he queried.

'But you heard Brad Henderson. He isn't going ahead with the custody battle—'

'Forget the custody battle!' Xander growled. 'Forget Brad Henderson! I'm talking about you and me. I'm—I'm attracted to you. And after yesterday evening I don't think you can deny your own response to me, either. Isn't that mutual attraction enough to be going on with?'

Casey stared at him, slightly stunned. Of course mutual attraction wasn't enough to base a marriage on. She already knew from being married to Sam how fleeting, how insubstantial that was—and surely Xander had learnt that lesson only too well himself from his years with Chloe. Long, bitter years, when there was neither love nor respect on either side.

As for mentioning that embarrassing time in his study last night…!

She couldn't quite meet the intensity of his gaze with her own as she answered him. 'Xander, if you haven't realised it yet, my marriage to Sam—the physical side of our relationship—was less than—satisfactory—'

'In what way?' Xander probed remorselessly.

'In every way,' she snapped back. 'He was my first and only lover before—before yesterday. And by the time my marriage ended I couldn't even bear to be in the same room with him, let alone have him touch me in that way. He was mocking and sarcastic about our—our sex-life. And I never—I never— It just never worked between the two of us,' she choked.

'What do you mean, mocking and sarcastic?' Xander asked more gently.

'Can't you guess?' Casey whispered. 'Sam never lost an opportunity to tell me how frigid, cold and unresponsive I was. How it was my own fault that I could never reach—that I never—' She looked up at Xander through tear-drenched eyes. 'Do I have to actually spell it out for you?' she cried.

No, she didn't have to spell anything out to Xander. Not Sam Bridges' deliberate cruelty to the young and inexperienced girl who had become his wife. Not the other man's years of emotional battering that had made it impossible for Casey to ever be able to relax enough with him to find release for her own pleasure.

A pleasure that Xander knew she'd had no problem reaching in *his* arms.

While he'd had her lying on a desktop!

He still cringed at the thought of how that must have seemed to Casey. Even more so now that he knew he had been the first man to ever give her physical pleasure.

'In the circumstances, I think it's totally wrong for the two of us to marry now that there's no reason for us to do so.' Casey's voice cracked emotionally, her eyes awash with unshed tears.

Tears that he had caused by his insensitivity. Tears that he wanted to kiss from her eyes. That he wanted to banish from her life for ever!

'Casey—'

'Don't, Xander!' she choked, as he would have reached out and grasped her arms. 'I don't want you to touch me again!' She turned away from him blindly. 'I will move my own and Josh's things out of here tomorrow, once I've taken him to school, and after that you need never see either of us ever again,' she added brokenly. 'Until then I think it would be better if we just stayed away from each other!'

'Casey, *please*—'

'No!' she told him forcefully, as he would have reached for her a second time. 'The last thing I need is your pity!'

Pity? Xander was too filled with a burning rage at Sam Bridges' complete callousness towards Casey, the lies he had told her in order to cover up his own inadequacies as a man, to be able to feel such a feeble emotion as *pity*. And he certainly didn't feel that emotion towards Casey...

Casey blinked her tears away as she looked up at Xander, able to see the same disgust and anger on his face she had so often seen on Sam's. 'See what a lucky escape you've had, Xander?' she whispered. 'I'm sure you no more want a frigid wife than Sam did.'

He shook his head in denial. 'You aren't frigid, Casey—'

'No?' she said scathingly. 'Then I must just be cold and un-responsive!' She squeezed her eyes shut. 'I have to go, Xander. I have to get out of here! I have to get away from you!' She turned quickly on her heel and fled the room.

CHAPTER THIRTEEN

SHE barely had time to close the bedroom door behind her before it was forced open again. She turned sharply to face Xander as he followed her into the room and closed the door firmly behind him to lean back against it.

'I told you—'

'I know what you told me,' he cut in softly. 'I heard every word that you said. Now I want you to listen to me for a few minutes, okay?'

She eyed him warily, but could see only warmth in that blue gaze now. His jaw was no longer clenched, and an encouraging smile was now curving those sculptured lips.

Her hands were fisted at her sides even as she swallowed hard before speaking. 'I don't see what else there is to say...'

'Don't you?' he breathed. 'Dear Lord, Casey, there is so much. So much! The first thing you need to know is that you are not any of the things Bridges told you that you were.'

'But—'

'*None* of them, Casey,' he insisted. 'You were a young girl of twenty when the two of you married, and Bridges was already in his late twenties; he was the one who should have been responsible for tenderly and lovingly introducing you to physical pleasure—'

'I really don't want to talk about this!' Casey groaned in embarrassment as she turned away. 'You didn't even want me enough last night to finish what you started!'

'Casey.' Xander spoke urgently from just behind her. 'Turn around and look at me. Please!'

She drew in a ragged breath, tensing her shoulders before turning to face him, keeping her gaze fixed firmly in the centre of his chest.

'Touch me,' he encouraged softly.

She raised startled eyes to look up at him, frowning with confusion, not knowing what he wanted of her.

Xander reached up and began to unbutton the black silk shirt he wore—slowly, taking his time over each button as he watched the play of emotions across Casey's oh-so-telling face. He saw the way her breath caught in her throat as the muscles of his chest and the flatness of his stomach were slowly revealed, the way the fiery colour caught and held in her cheeks as he pulled the shirt from his trousers and opened it.

'Touch me,' he repeated huskily.

She hesitated for only a moment, and then her hands moved up tentatively, lightly caressing as she touched the dark hair that grew on his chest, those caressing fingers leaving a trail of fire wherever she touched.

Xander held back none of his response to her slightest touch—his laboured breathing, his muscles clenching at her lightest caress. He practically stopped breathing altogether as her touch became bolder, moving silkily up the length of his chest, seeking, knowing, exploring each dip and curve of his flesh, until she finally pushed the shirt off his shoulders and down his arms, leaving him naked from the waist up. She came closer, not quite touching him as her hands moved along the taut width of his shoulders.

He wanted to be completely naked—wanted Casey's hands, her lips, to know all of him before she took him inside her and he let the warmth of her completely engulf him.

'Can you feel how I want you?' he groaned. 'Feel how *much* I want you!' He spoke more fiercely as he took one of her hands and placed it against him—against the throbbing heat of him.

Casey's eyes widened as she felt the outline of Xander's need. He was so big and hard, and as her hand ran the length of him she felt him surge at her lightest touch.

Xander *did* want her!

Now!

Urgently!

'Let me show you how far from frigid, cold and unresponsive you are,' Xander pleaded as his hands moved down to clasp hers within the warmth of his. 'Trust me, Casey,' he urged as she looked up at him uncertainly. 'Trust me not to hurt you. I promise I'll never do anything to hurt you. If I do anything—anything at all that you don't like—you have only to tell me and I'll stop, okay?'

'But—'

'We can talk later. We have all the time in the world to talk. Now I want to show you, to let you see, that you are the most sexy, arousing, erotically beautiful woman I have ever known.'

'But Chloe was so beautiful—'

'Chloe was an immoral alleycat!' Xander said harshly. 'I have absolutely no doubts that she and your husband were well matched, that they found together whatever it was they were looking for. But you, Casey…' His voice deepened to a husky growl. 'To me you're perfection. You are everything a woman should be. Beautiful. Warm. Kind. A loving, unselfish mother. With a body that is so incredibly, sexily, magnificently arousing that I only have to look at you to want to make love to you.' He drew in a ragged breath. 'I didn't stop last night because I didn't want you. I stopped because lovemaking should never be about taking, Casey, but about giving. And last night giving you pleasure was all that I needed or wanted.'

'And now?' Casey breathed softly.

'Now I would like us to make love to each other,' he told her, and he shed the rest of his clothes to stand before her completely naked. 'Slowly. Tenderly. Fiercely. I want us to love each other in every way there is between a man and a woman.'

'You really do want me?' she voiced shyly.

'Oh, Casey, how can you doubt it?' He took her hands in his and once more drew them to his body, his gaze holding hers as he slowly moved those hands across his chest, down the flatness of his stomach, and lower, placing them against him, around him, gasping as he allowed the fierce heat to flow through him. 'I think you may be a little overdressed for the occasion, though,' he murmured softly, and his arms moved about her and he slid the zip of her dress down her spine, before allowing the garment to fall to the carpeted floor.

Casey stood before him wearing only silky French panties and hold-up stockings, the style of her dress not having allowed for a bra. Her breasts were full and pouting—and begging for his kiss!

Casey's breath drew sharply in—and then stopped as she felt Xander's lips and tongue against her breasts, her back arching instinctively as she offered herself.

The bed was soft and welcoming as Xander laid her back upon it. His kisses and caresses were unrelenting in their intensity, and he shuddered his own pleasure as Casey caressed him in return, keeping nothing of his responses back as he allowed her the freedom to touch and kiss wherever she chose.

'Oh, God, Casey!' he moaned as her lips and tongue drove him mad. 'No more!' he finally gasped hotly, sitting up to lie her gently down beside him. 'Your turn now,' he promised, even as his mouth moved moistly, hotly, down the length of her body.

Casey lay before him unashamedly naked as he stripped the last of her clothes from her body. His lips and tongue tasted every inch of her, suckling and laving her breasts until she lay weak and gasping beneath him, and her cry was one of appeal as he moved lower and unerringly found the core of her, tasting her, savouring her, as he brought her to the very brink of release.

She looked up at him through half-closed lids as he moved up and above her, his weight on his arms as he settled between her thighs. Then he surged into the raw heat of her with slow, stroking thrusts.

She cried out hoarsely, her hands against the tautness of his spine as he moved harder and faster and her body convulsed around him. There was a look of pure rapture on Xander's face as he reached his own release.

'I could lie with you like this for ever,' Xander murmured some time later, his lips against her creamy throat, his arms tightly about her, their bodies still joined.

'So could I,' Casey acknowledged huskily, her hands lightly caressing his silky hair as it rested on his shoulders in tangled disarray.

Xander looked at her with intent blue eyes. 'I love you, Casey.'

Casey closed hers briefly, hardly able to believe he had said those words to her, before opening them and saying, 'Do you really, Xander?'

'More than life itself,' he vowed. 'Forget the past. Most of all, forget the cold-blooded way I asked you to marry me three weeks ago.' He groaned. 'As you've just seen, there is nothing in the least cold about the way you make me feel!'

Casey laughed softly, knowing a freedom with Xander that she had never experienced before. 'Or the way you make me feel,' she echoed huskily. 'I do love you—so very much, Xander.' She moved so that she could look down at him, careful not to dislodge him, loving the feel of him inside her, knowing him to be a part of her that was as necessary as breathing.

'Will you marry me, Casey?' Xander asked. 'For no other reason than because I love you. Because you love me. Will you, Casey?'

'I thought—before Brad arrived I believed you were going to tell me that you couldn't marry me, after all!' She breathed shakily, hardly able to believe that such happiness was really within her grasp.

'I was,' Xander confirmed. 'But only that I couldn't marry you under the conditions we had agreed,' he added quickly, as she frowned. 'I couldn't have been married to you and not wanted to be with you like this!' he told her fiercely. 'I would have been lying to you as well as myself if I had allowed us to sign that contract disclaiming any physical relationship between us. I want you too much, need you too much, to ever be able to agree to that!' he assured her gruffly. 'And I want, always, to give you the same honesty you've always given me,' he murmured, even as his hands moved to caress the softness of her hair. 'Marry me, Casey, and make me the happiest man that ever lived.'

'Oh, yes,' she said. 'Yes, I'll marry you, Xander!'

For a time there was only silence in the bedroom as they kissed each other with fierce hunger.

'When did you know that you loved me?' Casey finally asked wonderingly.

'I'm not completely sure of the exact moment I fell in love with you. But I knew for certain that it was love I felt for you when I looked at the contract last night after you left and saw that you refused to accept any money for yourself. You see, my darling, I had assumed you weren't happy with the contract because a million pounds wasn't enough—'

'Xander Fraser, I don't *want* your money—'

'I know that, my love.' He smiled. 'I know that only too well. But it seemed, after the way you left me last night, that you didn't want me, either.'

'How can you say that, after what happened?' Casey gasped incredulously.

'You seemed—unhappy that you had allowed it to happen.' He grimaced.

'I was stunned,' she corrected huskily. 'I really did believe that I was one of those women who simply don't enjoy the physical side of a relationship.'

'And now?' Xander teased.

'Now I would like us to make love again,' she admitted softly, even as she felt him stir inside her. 'In fact, I would like for us to stay in bed for a week, with absolutely no distractions but each other!'

'I think that might be arranged,' Xander muttered as he moved to kiss her. 'I'm sure the children won't mind if we ask Brad to stay with them while we disappear for a few days on our honeymoon.'

'We're really going to get married tomorrow, as planned?' Casey looked up at him with wondering eyes.

'I think perhaps we had better, don't you,' he said indulgently. 'I love you so much, Casey, and I'm not going to be able to keep my hands off you for some time to come.' His hand moved caressingly down the flatness of her waist to the silky curls beneath.

Love.

To have Xander love her.

To love Xander in return.

Love was what made all the difference…

CHAPTER FOURTEEN

'XANDER...?'

'Hmm?' he murmured sleepily against her throat, having fallen into a satiated sleep after their lovemaking.

Casey took a few moments for contented reflection before answering him.

Even after a year of marriage they still couldn't get enough of each other—of being together, of loving each other.

Xander often deferred business trips if Casey couldn't accompany him—something that wasn't always possible when they had two small children to think of. And Casey's late stage of pregnancy meant she hadn't been able to fly anywhere at all these last two months.

This last year of being Xander's wife, of uniting their two families—Brad had become grandfather to both Josh and Lauren—of making a child of their own, had been the happiest time Casey had ever known in her life.

And it was about to get better...

'I think we need to go to the clinic, Xander,' she told him softly.

'Hmm?' he murmured sleepily again. 'What?' he gasped, sitting up as her words penetrated his drowsy brain, with a panicked look on his face. 'Are you sure? Isn't it too early? The baby isn't expected for another couple of weeks!' he muttered worriedly, even as he got out of bed and began to pull on his clothes.

Casey gave a happy smile as she watched him put on his trousers without putting on his boxer shorts, and having to start all over again. 'I think the baby has decided otherwise,' she told him as she moved to the side of the bed.

'Fine.' He nodded distractedly, his hair a dark tangle as he ran an agitated hand through it. 'First I have to call Brad and get him to come and sit with Lauren and Josh. Then I have to—'

'Slow down, Xander.' Casey laughed. 'It isn't going to happen for hours yet,' she assured him. 'I just don't think it's going to wait until morning,' she added, as another contraction gripped her.

Xander paled and quickly crossed the bedroom to her side. 'You're going to be all right, aren't you, Casey?' he asked, gripping both her hands in his as he stared down at her intently. 'I couldn't bear it if anything happened to you—'

'Nothing is going to happen to me except that in a few hours' time we're going to have another son or daughter,' she said warmly.

Xander sat down on the bed beside her. 'I love you, Casey!' he told her fiercely. 'I love you, want you, and need you so very, very much!'

She leant forward and kissed him lingeringly on the lips. 'I love, want and need you in exactly the same way.' She straightened. 'Now, let's go and give birth to our son or daughter!' she added, with an exultant laugh.

Their daughter, Anna Louise, was born three hours later, with her father's glossy black hair and eyes of blue already tinged with her mother's green.

'I want half a dozen more,' Casey warned Xander as she watched the gentle way he cradled their daughter in his arms.

'Only half a dozen?' he teased, and he looked at her lovingly, an emotional catch in his voice.

Life was good—so very, very good, Casey acknowledged, even as her eyes began to close sleepily.

With Xander to love, and be loved by, she knew that it would always be that way…

* * * * *

LARGER-PRINT BOOKS!

HARLEQUIN *Presents*

PASSION
GUARANTEED
SEDUCTION

GET 2 FREE LARGER-PRINT NOVELS PLUS 2 FREE GIFTS!

YES! Please send me 2 FREE LARGER-PRINT Harlequin Presents® novels and my 2 FREE gifts (gifts are worth about $10). After receiving them, if I don't wish to receive any more books, I can return the shipping statement marked "cancel". If I don't cancel, I will receive 6 brand-new novels every month and be billed just $4.55 per book in the U.S. or $5.24 per book in Canada. That's a saving of at least 13% off the cover price! It's quite a bargain! Shipping and handling is just 50¢ per book.* I understand that accepting the 2 free books and gifts places me under no obligation to buy anything. I can always return a shipment and cancel at any time. Even if I never buy another book, the two free books and gifts are mine to keep forever.

176/376 HDN E5NG

Name _____ (PLEASE PRINT) _____

Address _____ Apt. #

City _____ State/Prov. _____ Zip/Postal Code

Signature (if under 18, a parent or guardian must sign)

Mail to the Harlequin Reader Service:
IN U.S.A.: P.O. Box 1867, Buffalo, NY 14240-1867
IN CANADA: P.O. Box 609, Fort Erie, Ontario L2A 5X3

Not valid for current subscribers to Harlequin Presents Larger-Print books.

**Are you a subscriber to Harlequin Presents books
and want to receive the larger-print edition?
Call 1-800-873-8635 today!**

* Terms and prices subject to change without notice. Prices do not include applicable taxes. Sales tax applicable in N.Y. Canadian residents will be charged applicable provincial taxes and GST. Offer not valid in Quebec. This offer is limited to one order per household. All orders subject to approval. Credit or debit balances in a customer's account(s) may be offset by any other outstanding balance owed by or to the customer. Please allow 4 to 6 weeks for delivery. Offer available while quantities last.

Your Privacy: Harlequin Books is committed to protecting your privacy. Our Privacy Policy is available online at www.eHarlequin.com or upon request from the Reader Service. From time to time we make our lists of customers available to reputable third parties who may have a product or service of interest to you. If you would prefer we not share your name and address, please check here. ☐

Help us get it right—We strive for accurate, respectful and relevant communications. To clarify or modify your communication preferences, visit us at www.ReaderService.com/consumerschoice.

HPLP10R

*Enjoy a sneak peek at fan favorite Molly O'Keefe's
Harlequin Superromance miniseries,*
THE NOTORIOUS O'NEILLS, *with*
TYLER O'NEILL'S REDEMPTION,
*available September 2010
only from Harlequin Superromance.*

Police chief Juliette Tremblant recognized the shape of the man strolling down the street—in as calm and leisurely fashion as if it were the middle of the day rather than midnight. She slowed her car, convinced her eyes were playing tricks on her. It had been a long time since Tyler O'Neill had been seen in this town.

As she pulled to a stop at the curb, he turned toward her, and her heart about stopped.

"What the hell are you doing here, Tyler?"

"Well, if it isn't Juliette Tremblant." He made his way over to her, then leaned down so he could look her in the eye. He was close enough to touch.

Juliette was not, repeat, *not* going to touch Tyler O'Neill. Not with her fingers. Not with a ten-foot pole. There would be no touching. Which was too bad, since it was the only way she was ever going to convince herself the man standing in front of her—as rumpled and heart-stoppingly handsome now as he'd been at sixteen—was real.

And not a figment of all her furious revenge dreams.

"What are you doing back in Bonne Terre?" she asked.

"The manor is sitting empty," Tyler said and shrugged, as though his arriving out of the blue after ten years was casual. "Seems like someone should be watching over the family home."

"You?" She laughed at the very notion of him being here for any unselfish reason. "Please."

He stared at her for a second, then smiled. Her heart fluttered against her chest—a small mechanical bird powered by that smile.

"You're right." But that cryptic comment was all he offered.

Juliette bit her lip against the other questions.

Why did you go?

Why didn't you write? Call?

What did I do?

But what would be the point? Ten years of silence were all the answer she really needed.

She had sworn off feeling anything for this man long ago. Yet one look at him and all the old hurt and rage resurfaced as though they'd been waiting for the chance. That made her mad.

She put the car in gear, determined not to waste another minute thinking about Tyler O'Neill. "Have a good night, Tyler," she said, liking all the cool "go screw yourself" she managed to fit into those words.

It seems Juliette has an old score to settle with Tyler.
Pick up TYLER O'NEILL'S REDEMPTION
to see how he makes it up to her.
Available September 2010,
only from Harlequin Superromance.

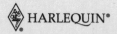
HARLEQUIN®

Showcase™

SHARON KENDRICK
Finn's Pregnant Bride

The Paternity Claim

On sale August 10, 2010

Reader favorites from the most talented voices in romance

Save $1.00 on the purchase of 1 or more Harlequin® Showcase™ books.